DESTINY

THE JOURNEY OF AN OFFICER

ASHISH DHATWALIA

Made with ♥ on the Notion Press Platform
www.notionpress.com

To my beloved family, steadfast pillars of support and endless inspiration. Your love and encouragement form the bedrock of my creative journey.

To my cherished friends, whose unwavering belief in this odyssey and shared adventures have made the path all the more meaningful.

To my mentors, grateful for the wisdom and guidance that have illuminated the way to this narrative.

To every dreamer and storyteller, may your tales kindle the flames of imagination for generations to come.

And to those who seek solace, embark on adventures, and find escape within the pages of a book, this endeavour is dedicated to you.

Contents

Foreword

It is with great admiration and respect that I pen this foreword for Captain Ashish's remarkable book. As a legal professional who values the narratives of resilience and leadership, I am particularly struck by the depth and richness of Captain Ashish's novel. His journey from the rigorous demands of military service to becoming an author is a compelling testament to the power of perseverance and vision.

In this book, Captain Ashish shares not only the strategic and operational insights of protagonist's military career but also the profound personal experiences that have shaped his life. Captain Ashish's narrative offers readers a rare glimpse into the disciplined world of an army officer, and more importantly, into the human side of a leader who has navigated the challenges of transition with remarkable grace and determination.

The account of his protagonist's transformation from an esteemed military career to a thriving entrepreneurial venture is both inspiring and instructive. Captain Ashish's novel is a celebration of the courage it takes to reinvent oneself and the tenacity required to succeed in a new arena. His ability to harness the skills and lessons from his military life into his business endeavors exemplifies the seamless integration of discipline and creativity.

What makes this book particularly engaging is Captain Ashish's candidness and the authenticity with which he shares the protagonist's experiences. From the heartwarming tales of protagonist's personal life to the insightful reflections on his professional journey, the author provides a narrative that is both deeply personal and universally relevant. The book is not just about achieving success but about understanding and embracing the journey that leads to it.

Advocate Shabnam Sharma
Legal Practitioner at Distt and Sessions Court Chandigarh

Preface

In the ever-changing landscape of life, there are stories that capture the imagination and inspire us to view the world through a different lens. This book is one such story—a testament to resilience, transformation, and the pursuit of dreams against all odds.

As I pen down these words, I am both humbled and exhilarated by the journey that has brought me to this point. From the disciplined life of an army officer to the unpredictable terrain of entrepreneurship, Shekhawat's path has been anything but ordinary. The narrative you are about to read is not merely a chronicle of his experiences; it is a reflection of the lessons learned, the victories won, and the love that shaped his life.

Shekhawat's life began in the rigorous discipline of military service, a phase marked by dedication, sacrifice, and a sense of duty. The army instilled in him the values that would guide his future endeavors and fueled a relentless drive for excellence. Yet, as with all journeys, there were moments of vulnerability and heartache that tested his resolve. It was during these times that he discovered not only his strength but also the power of love and resilience.

Transitioning from the army to the world of business was a leap that many might find daunting. The challenges were immense, but they were met with the same determination that defined my military career. The entrepreneurial journey was filled with trials and triumphs, and through it all, he remained committed to building something meaningful and impactful.

This book also delves into the personal aspects of his life, including the love that has been both a source of immense joy and profound lessons. His experiences in love and loss have been as transformative as his professional achievements, shaping his perspective and guiding his actions.

When Kate, an insightful and inquisitive journalist and author from California, reached out to him for an interview, he was both honored and excited. Her quest to understand the multifaceted nature of my journey brought forth a unique opportunity to share his story in its entirety. Through her questions and our conversations, they have explored not just the highlights of his career but also the deeper, more personal aspects that have shaped who he was today.

As you read these pages, I hope you find inspiration in the story of a man who navigated the complexities of military life, embraced the challenges of entrepreneurship, and sought meaning in love and relationships.

Thank you for joining me on this journey. May this book provide you with not only a glimpse into Shekhawat's world but also the motivation to forge your own path with courage and conviction.

Acknowledgements

Writing this novel has been an incredible journey, and it would not have been possible without the support, encouragement, and guidance of many wonderful people.

First and foremost, I would like to thank my family. To my parents, **Mr Surjeet Singh Dhatwalia** and **Mrs Neelam**, for always believing in me and encouraging me to follow my dreams. Your love and support have been my foundation. To my sister and brother in-law, **Advocate Shabnam Sharma** and **Major Ayush Sharma**, thank you for your unwavering patience, understanding, and for being my greatest cheerleader. Your belief in me kept me going even when I doubted myself.

I am deeply grateful to **MsRanju Thakur**, whose keen insights and tireless efforts helped shape this story into what it is today. Your feedback was invaluable, and your belief in my vision gave me the confidence to push forward.

A special thanks to my coursmates, **Captain Kartik Thakkar, Captain Shubham Singh, Captain Nikhil Chaudhary, Captain Naresh Kumar Yadav, Captain Ameer Navas, Captain Chandan, Captain Sunil Gora** and to my Junior **Captain Yashwardhan Singh Shekhawat**, who took the time to read early drafts and provided thoughtful and constructive feedback. Your input helped me see the story from different perspectives and refine it into something much stronger. Thank you for listening to me talk endlessly about characters, plot twists, and the writing process. Your enthusiasm and support were a constant source of motivation.

Lastly, I want to express my gratitude to all the readers out there. Your love for stories is what inspires me to write.

I hope this novel resonates with you and brings you as much joy in reading it as I had in writing it.

Thank you all for being a part of this journey.

Prologue

The quiet of the early morning was punctuated by the distant hum of an approaching helicopter. The sprawling villa nestled in the serene hills was slowly waking up, as the first rays of the sun began to filter through the dense foliage. Inside, the aroma of freshly brewed coffee mingled with the crisp, clean air, signaling the start of a new day.

Kate White, a journalist and a renouned author from California known for her in-depth interviews and captivating storytelling, had traveled thousands of miles to this remote corner of the world. Her mission was clear: to uncover the extraordinary journey of Major Yashwardhan Singh Shekhawat, a decorated army officer who had not only excelled in the military but had also carved out a remarkable career as an entrepreneur and author.

As Kate explored the villa, she marveled at the blend of old-world charm and modern luxury that defined Shekhawat's home. It was here, amidst the lush gardens and tranquil surroundings, that she would sit down with him to delve into the story of his life—a story that spanned from the rigorous discipline of the army to the innovative realms of business and literature.

The interview was set to begin at sunrise, a fitting time for Shekhawat to recount his past—a life filled with courage, love, and relentless ambition. Kate was eager to hear about his transformation from a respected military leader to a successful entrepreneur, and to understand the personal and professional experiences that shaped his journey.

As she was escorted to the golf course, where Shekhawat awaited, Kate was struck by the juxtaposition of the villa's formal elegance and the warm, personal touches that spoke of a life lived fully.

Shekhawat, now a man of distinction and accomplishment, greeted Kate with a mixture of humility and pride. His eyes, reflecting both the steely resolve of his military past and the thoughtful contemplation of his current ventures, held a promise of stories that would captivate and inspire.

As the interview commenced, Kate knew she was about to embark on a journey through the chapters of Shekhawat's life—each one a testament to his resilience, his passion for service, and his pursuit of excellence. The prologue of this narrative was set to unveil a life of extraordinary contrasts and compelling achievements, offering a glimpse into the heart of a man who had mastered both the art of war and the craft of business.

In this quiet, secluded villa, with the morning sun casting its first light, Kate was ready to explore the depths of Major Yash Shekhawat's story—one that promised to be as enlightening as it was inspiring.

CHAPTER ONE

The Interview

In the crisp December air, the small town in the outskirts of Shimla transformed into a picturesque, idyllic landscape. The sky was a clear expanse, and the cheerful chirping of birds filled the air. Major Shekhawat stood in the middle of his expansive 18-hole parkland golf course. Ducks gathered by a water puddle, seeking solace from the gentle, warming sunlight. Shekhawat observed the scene with his left hand resting on his waist and his right palm shielding his eyes from the bright rays of the sun.

As time flowed, the tranquility was interrupted by a growing noise. A chopper was approaching, struggling against the cool December breeze. It descended rapidly and gracefully touched down on the helipad marked on the golf course, not far from where Shekhawat stood. A woman in her early thirties, a foreign national, elegantly clad in a knee-length black dress and three-inch pumps, stepped out of the chopper.

Shekhawat, along with two other men, braved the gusty wind and approached to welcome the lady. She greeted them with a warm smile.

"Good Morning, Ms. White. Welcome to my place. I hope you had a comfortable journey," Shekhawat greeted her, shaking her hand.

"Good Morning, Major Shekhawat. I'm truly grateful for the courtesy of sending the chopper," the lady replied with a hint of seriousness.

"The pleasure is all mine, Ms. White. Please have some water, and then I'll escort you to your accommodations for the next few days," Shekhawat gestured toward a nearby suite. The butler standing beside Shekhawat offered her a glass of water.

"You can simply call me by my first name, Major," Kate smiled.

"Can we skip the accommodations for now, Major? Without wasting any time, I want to start interviewing you. I want to cover your story ASAP. Let me tell you, it's great to see you face to face," Kate exclaimed while sipping water from her glass. She was eager to initiate the interview.

"Sure, Kate, in whatever way you prefer," Shekhawat guided her to a shaded area with two chairs and a round table.

"So, Major Shekhawat, how does it feel to be the CEO of one of India's tech giants?" Kate, a prolific author, began the interview.

"Honestly, it feels more accomplished to be sitting in front of one of the finest authors, Kate," Shekhawat responded humorously. They both shared a chuckle.

"First and foremost, thank you for coming to my place. It's awesome to be the founder of a leading tech giant in the country's technology sector," Shekhawat added with a broad smile. The conversation took place in Shekhawat's golf course, adjacent to his villa in the suburbs of Shimla.

"How did you achieve so much at such a young age?" Kate inquired.

"I'd say it's not that young, being thirty-seven. In comparison to other billionaires like Zuckerberg, Jobs, and

Gates, I'm rather late," Shekhawat teased.

"Compared to them, yes, but it's not as old as it might seem," Kate added.

Major Shekhawat, the founder of Graviton, was being interviewed by Kate White, an author representing a leading publishing house, to cover his life journey.

"Risks! I would say. I took risks, failed, tried again and failed again, then tried again, and failed again. Trust me; I've reached this stage because of my 'try again' philosophy. I'm still failing today. Failing is the art that has shaped me over time and continues to teach and mold me," Shekhawat explained.

"Why did you leave the army? You could have excelled there too," Kate inquired.

"I never left the army. I still work for the organization," Shekhawat chuckled.

"Oh, I see," Kate responded, slightly taken aback.

"Tell me, what's the story behind the name Graviton?" Kate asked with curiosity.

"Graviton is considered a particle responsible for gravitational force, similar to photons being responsible for light. It's yet to be discovered. By naming my company after it, I felt like I did my part," Shekhawat chuckled, and they both laughed.

"Ah, now I've got you," Kate added with a laugh.

"Well, jokes aside, I actually liked the name. It sounded unique. Fun fact: other tech names like Luminous, Photon, Pixel, were already taken by other firms," Shekhawat explained.

"Great. It does sound unique. Now, about your personal life. Any plans for marriage?" Kate inquired with a broad smile.

"Marriage. I think it's a construct by conventional society. I'm more comfortable living alone. You have the freedom to enjoy the lifestyle you want, on your terms, and feel the fresh air around you rather than living in a stale environment until death or feeling dejected after a divorce or separation," Shekhawat offered his perspective.

"Opinions vary, and yes, yours is logical. Many couples do lead happy lives too," Kate added.

"You never know, Kate, what's beneath the quilt, what's the story hidden behind those smiles," Shekhawat replied.

"That was an intense thought. It seems like you're a heartbroken Major," Kate observed.

"Apparently," Shekhawat acknowledged with a brief laugh.

"So, what's your story? Was there a lady or ladies?" Kate inquired with a cunning smile.

"It's not the lady I was in love with, rather 'time.' I fell in love with time, and I cherish many of those memories until today. Memories are memories, sweet or bitter; it doesn't matter. What really matters is how you embrace them," Shekhawat reflected, lost in thought. There was a brief silence, and Shekhawat realized he was delving deep into his memories.

"Well, it would take a lot of time to unfold my story, Kate. It's not an event I can recite. It's a series of events that led to one thing or another, many ups and downs, joys and sorrows, like a roller coaster of emotions," Shekhawat explained with a genial smile.

"That's precisely why I'm here to interview you. Why don't we start with your army career first?" Kate suggested, encouraging Shekhawat to share his military experiences.

"Sure, Kate, that sounds fine," Shekhawat agreed and began narrating his journey.

"Why did you join the army when you wanted to become a tech entrepreneur?" Kate asked curiously.

"I never wanted to be a tech entrepreneur. I never planned for it. I was passionate about joining one of the elite services of the country, and I did. The military made me the man I am today. I could never have been like this if I were not a part of the military," he replied emotionally, and Kate sensed the depth of his feelings.

"So, what made you say that, Major?" Kate asked with a curious smile.

"The military taught me punctuality, life, friendship, decisiveness, maturity, and everything else you can think of that defines a gentleman in society. It's not just me; all the other men who were with me are more or less on the same path," Shekhawat explained.

"Fascinating. Please continue with your story," Kate urged, clearly captivated by his confident demeanor.

"I was the third generation in the army, but the first officer in all three generations. We didn't have any known army officers in our family. Becoming a military officer was a primary goal in my bucket list. As a child, born and raised in an army environment, the army uniform always fascinated me," he continued.

"Sounds interesting," Kate nodded with a smile.

"It's indeed much more. Let me start unfolding my training phase, so you can understand how interesting it was," Shekhawat chuckled.

Meanwhile, a butler entered and placed a tray of snacks and juice on the table.

"That seems like a fantastic idea – having snacks here with the cold breeze, you and me basking in the sun and me listening to your story," Kate commented with a cheerful tone.

"Yes that is scenic, Kate you must be hungry," Shekhawat added, offering Kate the juice and snacks while holding his own glass.

Meanwhile, they observed other servants carrying her belongings from the chopper toward the guest room.

CHAPTER TWO

The Training Phase

On the 5th of June at 0500 hrs, our train pulled into Gaya station. The zenith of summer had shrouded Gaya in humidity. At the youthful age of nineteen, excitement surged within me, anticipating the commencement of a new chapter at the Officers Training Academy in Gaya. Kartik, my comrade from the Service Selection Board (SSB) process, disembarked alongside me. Stepping off the train, we found ourselves amidst a sea of others, seemingly disoriented until we spotted a cohort of army personnel making their way towards us.

We observed robust army personnel donning a red sash diagonally running from their shoulder to waist, adorned with the crest of the Officers Training Academy. It became clear later that these stalwart individuals were our drill instructors, tasked with guiding us to the army buses stationed just outside the railway station and overseeing our conduct throughout the training phase at the academy.

The sensation of finally living my dream was truly beyond words. It's challenging to articulate that overwhelming feeling. It felt as though I had accomplished everything in my life, leaving me pondering what more I could aspire for.

We boarded the bus together, and it took us the next two to three hours to reach the place that each one of us sitting inside the bus had always dreamt of and eagerly awaited. Meanwhile, we observed huts scattered everywhere, revealing a lack of proper sewage system—a clear sign of administrative shortcomings in that area. Gaya was underdeveloped at that time, and the overall view was quite disheartening.

At last, the bus entered a spacious gateway—the entrance to the Officers Training Academy territory. The moment we disembarked, the seniors—by seniors, I refer to the second-termers, six months senior to our course—guided us to our respective company areas. We were assigned individual rooms, and in the very next moment, we were instructed to gather in the open area within the company premises.

Next, we had our haircuts. After which all of us were looking almost similar, it was a buzz cut.

In the formation of- three ahead and rest behind, we were guided in front of the adjutant's office. Standing quietly on the lush green lawn infront of the office barracks we all were quiet and were keeping to ourselves since we didn't know each other much. In the next few minutes a well-built man was standing infront of us. He was in his horse riding rig and addressed all of us-

Good Morning Gentlemen

Welcome to the academy. Congratulations to each of you for making it this far. From here on, you all will embark on a journey travelled only by the valiant ones. The life that you have chosen for yourselves will be full of ups and downs. This is not meant to demotivate you but to prepare you mentally for what lies ahead on your journey. Upcoming days are going to be challenging for all of you. You will undergo training in soldiering and camaraderie. Each one of you is expected to exhibit the utmost discipline, and any necessary refinement will be taken care of by the ustads (Drill Instructors) standing next to you.

I also guarantee that upon your passing out from this academy, you will emerge as the most formidable soldiers and exemplary gentlemen. Wishing each of you the best of luck for journey ahead. Remember, you are neither the first nor the last to pass out from this academy.

These were his words and they still echo my ears. With this the adjutant marched off to his office.

The next few days started with a slow progression. Slowly and gradually the pace of the training increased and we could feel the heat of training around us.

When you're in the Officers Training Academy, you race against time, and that's what most of us experienced, myself included. The initial three months were challenging. There was a Bollywood movie that resonated with many of us - 'Lakshya'.

Unlike that movie, training wasn't at all the length of a song, which, again, most of us used to listen to," Shekhawat chuckled, and Kate joined in too.

"So, it was tough?", Kate asked him.

"Apparently, but later it became a part of the four years journey", Shekhawat replied.

"Sorry to bother you; please feel free to add on," Kate added in an apologetic tone.

"Alright. We were totally absorbed in the training schedule at the academy. Morning started at six for the physical training followed by classes in the academic's block at eight, soon after the breakfast. One class after the another with sleep-thirst eyes. Weapon training, tactics, army administration and logistics and many more subjects like this.

Studying non-medical during school days and then making an abrupt shift to an entirely new domain didn't work very well for me. I found myself struggling, particularly in military subjects, and was on the verge of failing in almost all of them.

I still recall a particular instance when we were taking a tactics exam (science of warfare), and I couldn't grasp a single concept, ultimately scoring only one mark out of fifty. That same evening, my DS (Officer Instructor) approached me in the company area (cadets' accommodation) and inquired about how I ended up with such a low score.

Believe me, I got goose bumps. An instructor approaching a cadet during unofficial hours suggested that something significant might have occurred.

I had no reply and luckily managed an easy escape somehow. From there, I got the primal lesson of army and that was to manage the studying time and score better marks to avoid any troubles.

Fortunately, I cleared all my PT (Physical Training) tests in first attempt and was the only one in my course to achieve such a milestone. Physicals are amongst the important things and an integral part of basic military training. This made my sail smooth and easy in OTA.

We also had drill classes, and believe me, drill is the most daunting aspect of training. In every drill session, you had to drive your heel a few inches extra into the ground to convince the drill instructors that it had touched the surface of the earth. There was a parade ground where the drill period took place daily, and passing the drill test was a prerequisite for earning the privilege of liberty outside (an out pass for a day).

There is a very funny incident happened with me", Shekhawat immediately recollected an anecdote.

"What funny incident?", Kate with a sudden curious look asked.

"DLTGH stands for Days Left To Go Home... and one fine day while I was heading towards the academics block from the cadet's mess on my bicycle, a senior termer stopped me and asked me-

'What's the DLTGH left?'. To which I immediately blurted out, 'forty days sir'. Following, he said-

'Seems like you are in very hurry to go home...' and the next word I heard was 'BIKES UP...' till academics block I was BIKES UP. In the academy, bicycles are called bikes.

"After a week, during the study period hours in the evening time, my overstudy (a senior termer responsible for individual's discipline) walked up to my room. He inquired about my studies when suddenly he brought up the topic of DLTGH.

I gave a very peculiar look as if I am unaware of the count... The very next moment I was legs up and hands down with wall supporting my feet in my room", Shekhawat laughed.

"Either way, you were in for trouble," Kate concluded with a laugh.

"Yes, that's the irony of knowing and not knowing in the army. If you know, you'll be screwed; if you don't, you'll be screwed royally," Shekhawat laughed.

Somehow, the first term (six months) came to an end, and before heading for our term break, we had a jungle lecture-cum-demonstration. We were taught the basic tactics of surviving in the jungle. Firstly, we learned how to catch a snake and how to barbecue it, followed by various other creatures. Towards the end, while the instructor was holding a hen in his bare hands, he asked us, 'Who wants me to chop its head with my hands?' Some of us raised our hands, excluding me. Instructor performed it infront of us. We all were flabbergasted to see him doing it with bare hands. Negi was one of the smartest coursemates we had. He was sitting next to me.

'for the next stunt we both will raise our hands and let's see who gets the cake...', he exclaimed in a very excited yet enthusiastic tone that somehow convinced me. I was ok with that.

'Who wants me to slit the throat with my teeth?' the green beret instructor asked. As per the deal, I raised my hand, and when I looked around, it was just me, not even Negi. He backed out at the last moment. I was naive. I felt like I had been played.

'Yeah... you jackass. Help yourself', the green beret handed over me the hen or cock I don't know what that heck was. I had to slit it the way told.

The second term had to start and now we were supposed to be the senior most in the academy, since there were only two terms at Officers Training Academy.

The second term went really well, and I performed satisfactorily in both academics as well as weapon and physical training.

I recall a night at the camp, somewhere in the outskirts of Gaya district, Bihar. The landscape was desolate and barren. The entire day was chaotic as we scoured for a coursemate's lost weapon. Exhausted, we finally found it near a water stream past midnight.

Observing our low morale and the strange silence, our instructor, Major Don summoned us in front of him. He enlightened us on the significance of the control store issued by the military. It was a life lesson, emphasizing that soon we would bear stars on our shoulders and shoulder significant responsibilities. Major Don further added that we are serving this motherland and a soldier should never be sad and possess a low morale. To motivate us and to boost our morale he himself sang the song, a song that my ears will never forget and the echoes of the song still resonate in my ears. It was the IMA (Indian Military Academy) song".

"That was a bold encounter", Kate sighed.

"Indeed", Shekhawat replied immediately.

"So, this was all about your training, right? And after this you joined military college?", Kate further added.

"I didn't join military college. It was the next step in the ladder. Since I have lost all of my touch from the studies so out of three military colleges located at three different places, Pune was my first priority. This priority was not based on the engineering I wanted to do rather based on the city life and exposure it could provide. The rest two were located in nearly remote locations as compared to College of Military Engineering, Pune. Cadets liked Pune due to many reasons, the prime of which was the ball night that only military college at Pune offered", Shekhawat explained in a thrilling tone.

"Sorry to interrupt you, but what is this ball night exactly?", Kate interrupted Shekhawat and was curious to know regarding the ball.

"It's akin to a prom night, where in the cadets have the liberty to call their girlfriends for a couple dance, followed by certain prize distributions such as best couple and all...", Shekhawat answered her curiosity.

"So, finally I landed up in military college Pune. The toughest part was training and studies together and this time it was not about service subjects only. The engineering syllabus too was fused into the curriculum. Good part was, the count of army instructors reduced and there were hardly a handful of them. The bitter truth was the syllabus was too much. I was least interested in studying engineering, but I didn't have any choice. Frankly speaking, I never wanted to do engineering.

Now we had five terms (semesters, each consisting of six months) over us, which meant we had many senior termers above us and trust me it was a nightmare. You have to take every step very carefully to avoid getting into unnecessarily troubles, causing future hassles for you.

I failed in three subjects in my first phase tests of the first term (semester) of engineering and was the only one to manage such a fortune. The next was, my PCC (Platoon Cadet Captain, a sixth termer, the senior most term) came to know and he was annoyed as I was part of Alpha platoon and we were known for our academics and I felt as if I am the one letting the whole platoon down, but later I came to know there were many other seniors too in the crime and I literally laughed at myself. But, failing in three subjects added only miseries to my life in the military college. Now, I was grilled more by my seniors and many a time called during the breakfast timings too", Shekhawat was nostalgic now.

"So that meant skipping meals?", Kate added.

"Sometimes yes", Shekhawat added

"had been a tough time, I guess", Kate further added.

"Was a time. But it made me mentally strong enough to face the challenges that God was preparing for me. The irony was that I topped in those three subjects in the finals and was the only one in the whole Cadets Training Wing (CTW), where we were getting trained, to top in three subjects", Shekhawat smiled.

"Must have been proud? By the way, what is this military college and CTW relation", Kate asked.

"CTW which stands for Cadets Training Wing is a faction of military college. It is especially meant for cadets, where they are trained and educated simultaneously", Shekhawat cleared her query.

"Alright"

Kate smiled.

"I like your smile Kate", Shekhawat chuckled.

"Thank you. Now, let's back to your side", Kate replied with a smile on her face.

"Yeah. Time passed and I graduated my three consecutive terms and finally landing into the fourth one. My fourth term was a gobsmacking and a turning point in my life that actually shaped me as the visionary everyone see me today. This was the term where we were allotted our specific streams of engineering. Civil engineering was the priority over mechanical since there was a myth amongst us- mechanical is a tough thing. I, too, opted for civil engineering but got casualty to mechanical domain. I was the only one left in whole Alpha platoon in my course which comprised Naresh and Nikhil and now I had no group to study with. I thought I will flunk now for sure and I did... again in one of the subjects but luckily managed to sail through in the finals", Shekhawat laughed.

"So, this was the turning point, getting motivation from your failures?", Kate was confused.

"No, a small incident happened to me. There was a senior of mine who used to come to my cabin every 1400 hrs after lunch and used to screw me for some of my blunders which I will cover subsequently with you. So, one fine noon I was just lying half dead on the bed and I closed my eyes and out of nowhere I imagined that in next two minutes the senior will come and he will be wearing a white t-shirt and black shorts and will kick my door. To my shock cum surprise things exactly happened in the same way as I thought and I was glad to see that though he was punishing me but I predicted everything exactly the same. For a moment I thought I have attained a spiritual prophecy and trust me this was the beginning, beginning to many things altogether that will shape my future. Later that night I came to my room and took out my smartphone. Smartphones were strictly banned but I managed it somehow from my second term itself and never got caught by any of the seniors ever", Shekhawat was remembering his long-gone faded memories.

"That night I searched for the future prediction thing. All I could find was Artificial Intelligence. I probed it deeper and found it quite fascinating. But frankly speaking I had no coding background and it required coding knowledge. I felt very helpless as we didn't have access to the internet officially. There was a computer lab in the Wing but that too was only allowed once a week. We were doing engineering but we were not doing engineering. I used to read from the soft copies in the night time and used to imagine that after a year or so I will have the liberty to access internet and start with the actual coding stuff. Time-being, I developed a new knack of learning languages and I started with Spanish. Whatever free time I could manage, I used to practice Spanish a lot and made a target that I will by the end of training, learn it completely which I did", Shekhawat was nostalgic and proud at the same time.

"So you know Spanish?", Kate asked.

"Pashto, Mandarin, Hangul, Urdu, Punjabi and Ladakhi also", Shekhawat added proudly.

"I am impressed man. You are a genius", Kate was impressed.

"Talking of genius, I remember, in my fourth term itself I discovered that I am an ambidextrous and can write simultaneously with both my hands. One hand, writing a mirror image to the other hand. This stunned me and later I came to know that there are a bunch of people in the entire world who can do this. This acted as a catalyst in imbuing more confidence and believe in myself more than ever before. I actually realised my worth. But still it didn't help me to become a topper and I never wanted to be one. I believe that writing on a piece of paper and getting happy over seeing scoring good marks was a scam, a scam that we do to ourselves. Creating something out of scratch by the application of theoretical knowledge fascinated me always", Shekhawat added.

"True. The real essence of education is application and not scoring marks on sheets. Later on, nobody cares about those sheets. It is more like that a piece of paper is defining your qualifications", Kate supported Shekhawat.

"You can do that?", Kate asked curiously.

"Do what?", Shekhawat asked.

"that thing... writing with both hands simultaneously", Kate added.

"I guess that's what I have told you", both of them laughed.

"Wow... this is crazy. Trust me, I have never met a person like you ever before", Kate was impressed by Shekhawat's brilliance.

"Kate, I think this is enough for today. Let's have lunch. I will narrate the rest of my side on the dinner table. Will that be fine?", Shekhawat requested her.

"That's alright. It is your story, you're the narrator. So, whatever you say. I guess still I have few more days here, which will be enough to make you unfold your side", Kate winked with a smile. Shekhawat responded in affirmation.

Both of them headed inside the villa. Shekhawat escorted Kate to the dining hall which had a fire place too. It was a classic 70s setup, aristocratic to be precise.

… the continuation

...the continuation

"The ambience is good", Kate exclaimed.

"Indeed...", Shekhawat replied in a low tone.

"So, who all you have in your family?", Kate asked further.

"Me and my daughter Vani only", Shekhawat replied in an emotional tone.

"But you are unmarried as far as I am aware", Kate was confused.

"My friend's daughter. He is no more...", it was an emotional moment for Shekhawat. There was a pause for a minute or more.

"Sorry to hear that Major. How old is she?", Kate came closer to him and rested one of her hands on his shoulder, while Shekhawat was sitting.

"She is ten. That's ok... ups and downs are a part of life", Shekhawat gathered himself and replied to Kate.

"Ramveer Lunch lagaao madam ke liye", Shekhawat asked his butler Ramveer who was probably in his early forties to prepare the dining table for lunch. After having lunch for around half an hour Shekhawat stood up. He seemed to be in a bit hurry.

"Kate, will catch you up after a nap", Shekhawat requested Kate to excuse him for a nap.

"Sure...", while Kate was still chewing her food.

"Ramveer Madam ko Guest room me le jaana", and subsequently ordered Ramveer to escort Kate to the Guest room once she is done with her lunch.

"Catch you up in the evening Kate", Shekhawat took an off and headed towards the basement stairs.

Kate waved him off and both of them parted.

Shekhawat went to the basement and was there till evening, probably figuring out something there.

"Sahab, madam aapke bare me puch rahi hain", Ramveer came down to the basement hall and informed Shekhawat that Kate was asking his whereabouts.

"Tum chalo main aata hoon", Shekhawat informed his butler that he will be at Kate's location soon.

It was winter's time and the temperature was dropping rapidly. As evening progressed further, the landscape was bathed with eternal glow of moonlight, casting long shadows of the glistening snow. The green landscape was covered with beautiful white snow topping. The air was carrying the whispers of the season through the surroundings. As dusk decended, the enchantment deepend gradually.

Kate was sitting in the porch of the villa and was lost into her own thoughts when Shekhawat suddenly interrupted.

"Liking it?", Shekhawat smiled at Kate.

"Yeah… it is so beautiful and satisfactory at the same to see snowflakes slowly settling down on the earth while travelling all the way from heavens. Where were you?", Kate was glad to be there.

"Oh… I was at the basement", Shekhawat replied.

Kate was wearing a knee length white skirt and a denim jacket on top. Kate was a blonde. Shekhawat was wearing a black blazer upon a pathaani kurta-pyjama and a pakhol (afghani head gear) was covering his skull. It was a typical afghani attire. He liked wearing that.

"Major, you have a charming personality. Didn't you ever fall for anyone?", Kate was holding a coffee mug in both of her hands.

"To wit, I was not like this before, I was more of a guy whom girls generally don't prefer interacting with",

Shekhawat sat next to her while clasping a coffee mug from Ramveer's tray.

"…I tried calling her many times from the academy. Every time I called, she didn't pick and when she called to enquire about the unknown number which was of-course mine flashing on her screen, I was in my classes.

This is when I was at officers training academy and she was at her engineering college in the south of the mainland. One fine day, probably the last week before our passing out, there was a variety show organised for all passing out cadets. Our families too were invited. Mine didn't come because of some reasons which I am not able to recall right now. That day in between the show, I received a call and it was her number flashed up on the screen. I got excited. She asked me who I am and I told her my name.

'Yash why did you call me so many times?', it was Meera.

'I wanted to tell you something Meera...', I was literally very hopeful that now she might say yes to my proposal.

'yes... I am listening', Meera added.

'Meera... I like you from school days. Never told you before, but I was always in love with you', I was so naïve, barely an adult.

'And when did this happen...?', that was not a very welcoming one coming from her side. She was rude.

'...from school days', I was very straightforward and least of a shy this time.

'I already have a boyfriend dude. Go find someone else of your match', with this she disconnected. I tried calling her again but she blocked my number. I was hurt and badly hurt. I talked to myself and asked- isn't it enough. Now that I am almost an officer, why is she still avoiding me", Shekhawat was sipping coffee and was probably staring at the white landscape that was created by the snowflakes.

"I feel bad... for her now", she laughed, breaking the silence.

"She missed an opportunity. Probably a life time opportunity of knowing a genius like you Major", Kate further added.

"Apparently", Shekhawat gazed at her and joined her with a smile.

"So, how did it start? If you don't mind sharing...", Kate was eager to know the whole plot from beginning.

CHAPTER THREE

The Saga

"'Shekhawat get out of there... hurry up man', a boy shouted out loudly standing away from the scuffle which was going on outside the school's main gate.

I looked at my back and I could see fifteen odd guys running towards my direction. I was frightened. Two or three I could handle but fifteen... NO CHANCE!

Without wasting a single breath, I gathered myself ASAP and ran towards Nitin's direction, somehow escaped and saved myself for that day. 'Army School' was my school, located in the heart of Jaipur city. I was in the tenth standard, a typical teenager full of anger and regular school fights was my teenage syllabus. But this fight I had for Meera. Meera was the girl I was in deep love with. Meera recently joined our school, she was studying at Delhi previously. Her father was a serving Colonel. The day she entered the class, she made a huge impact on everyone, especially the boys. Her fluency over the English language attracted most of us. But what really attracted me towards her was her modesty and confidence. Unlike other girls, she used to talk to everyone and was hardly a shy. She was intelligent, beautiful and smart. It was a co-ed school where in boys and girls had different rows inside classroom.

Somehow my father came to know about the school fight and when he got to know the reason was a girl, I was beaten to death. He warned me, 'listen up chap, the next time if I get any complaints from any of your teachers, I swear to God, I will kill you myself. School is for education and not for making love'. My father was in a Rajput Battalion (part of Infantry Regiment of Indian Army). I quietly went to the room. It was beautiful. I was in love with that time. She was all I could think about in those days. I was in love with the time.

One thing that remained consistent was my scores. I was a science enthusiast. Physics, chemistry and mathematics were my favourite subjects and I loved applying them in real day to day life. When I was in class ninth, I made a smoke bomb and very excitedly told my chemistry teacher about the same, unaware of the shock she will be in for the next couple of days. The very next day my father was summoned up to the school and I was counselled to the brims. The worst part was that though I loved applying science but after that incident I used to think that applying science is a trash and it is more important to score good marks in exams if you want to become successful in life. I was naïve.

'Why do you ask so many questions Yashvardhan?', it was the last class and I was winding up my stuff when she, bag slung on her back, asked me with a smile over her face.

'Because I...' I shrugged my shoulders. That was the time I too realised 'why'. I could not say anything because I had literally nothing to say. She was very beautiful and I kept looking at her for seconds.

'Add on', she added. 'I don't know', she made me nervous and I replied without pondering much. I was a shy. The fact was, it was only me who was in love.

Mahesh Nagar was the tuition hub of Jaipur. Though fantastic in science, I too joined tuition just to get an extra glimpse of her. I used to cycle around 10 kms from home to tuition centre just to see her. Some memories I still have. One such was the day when she was just sitting besides me and the room where our class used to happen was a snug as compared to the strength of students it accommodated. It was winters evening and was quite a cold outside. The teacher was teaching on the board and all of my focus was on her. The most attractive part of her was her eyes. And that day she actually talked to me.

'Hey when did you join the tuition?'

'It's been a month', I replied feeling butterflies all over.

'Really?'

'Yeah'.

This was the longest conversation we had actually. I still remember she used to come by a white Maruti Gypsy, with a soldier driving it all the way from her home to the school and tuition centre. She used to appear like a princess when she used to step out of the Gypsy. This was also one of my motivations to join army and someday walk up to her dad and ask her out for a date.

We live an ideal life in our imaginations until reality strikes us apart. That was my case. My father was an OR (Other Rank) in the army, while her father was a senior colonel. The gap between our worlds was vast. By the time we reached 12th grade, the final year of school, she became the house prefect and probably started dating the head boy of the school. I felt terrible and jealous. Attending tuitions was just an excuse to see her, but seeing her with someone else, laughing and talking, only added to my suffering. I could not accept the fact that she was actually dating someone else instead of me.

I used to imagine that someday I will become an army officer and she will be mine forever and this used to make me feel very happy. So, becoming an officer was the primal goal I had. But as I said an ideal life only exist in our imaginations and mine too was not a very different case here.

Many a times I tried talking to her but honestly speaking I was hesitant, used to feel shy and nervous at the same time. One day after school while she was standing outside the main gate of the school I went near to her.

'Hi Meera are you waiting for someone?'

'Oh... hi Yash. Yes... waiting for George', she replied with a courteous smile. I too smiled back and with a light gesture whisked away from the site.

It was mid-year time, school fest was organised by the newly appointed principal, which gave enough time to the non-participants to chitchat around in the class since most of the teachers and participants were busy in preparations.

It was a group of six students, girls and boys mixed and we were playing truth and dare. So, the pen pointed towards me and the other end was at Meera.

'So... TRUTH Or DARE?', she asked.

'truth', I said.

'So, here's the thing... what is your aim in life?'

We were kids back then and trust me the level of questioning and dares was too cliché unlike today.

'I want to become an army officer', I replied immediately.

'You don't have that personality Yashvardhan...trust me...', everyone laughed and since she was laughing, I too joined them.

'I am seriously telling you Yash', she added and there was a pause.

I felt bad but I ignored and we continued playing. Daughter of a senior army officer telling me this meant something, something I need to work upon. I took it positively though.

After a few pen-rotations, it was her turn and one of the girls sitting besides me asked her to choose one out of truth and dare.

'Truth', she replied.

'Whom do you like amongst boys in our class and why?', the girl asked.

'Ok honestly speaking... I like George because he seems classy, confident and a focussed guy, even today also, he is busy helping teachers in the fest preparations', she replied with a blush over her face. Now, this was the last nail in the coffin.

The world like people who are confident, focussed and ambitious. This was all I could draw out from her reply and the fact that she considered George better than me. I was jealous and hurt at the same time.

Although it should not be the case, but belonging to a class far below to hers used to make me feel low always in front of her and her friend circle, which generally comprised of rich guys and girls. I wanted to be a SOMEONE now. Someone she could feel proud to be with. NDA entrance exams were looming over the horizon and I was not at all prepared. That year I appeared twice for the examination but was not fortunate enough to make it through the merit. The next month boards results were out and this time I was lucky to score a 95% aggregate in my Physics, chemistry and maths subjects.

The school was over now and since it was a board examination so there was no parents-teacher meet, which meant no seeing her anymore. She was lost now.

The next step was informing my parents about my decision to take coaching for the NDA examination. Following our plan, I went to Chandigarh and enrolled in a coaching center. However, after a week, I was utterly fed up and couldn't find the motivation to study. With college admissions at Delhi University starting the following month, I needed to make a decision quickly. I called my parents and told them I was dropping out of the coaching program. Though they were not pleased, they supported my decision", Shekhawat narrated a past memory.

CHAPTER FOUR

Nostalgia

Before joining the officers' training academy, the last time I heard from her was when I was in Delhi. I called her once. She had enrolled in one of the finest engineering colleges in the South and was pursuing a Bachelor's degree. I dialed her number.

"Hi, Meera, Yashvardhan here," I said excitedly.

"Who... Yashvardhan?" Her response immediately dampened my enthusiasm.

"Yashvardhan Singh Shekhawat... from Army School Jaipur."

"Oh... hi Yashvardhan... It's been a long time. How are you? And where are you these days?" Her tone was formal, almost distant. I felt a pang of disappointment.

"I'm in Delhi, studying at Delhi University," I replied, matching her tone, trying not to let my excitement show.

"Hey Yashvardhan, I'm a bit occupied. Can we talk later? I'm really sorry," she said, her apology sounding rehearsed. Trust me, I felt bad. But that was okay—after all, it was only me who was crazy about her. She never felt the same, so I shouldn't have raised my hopes or expected much from her.

Now, I was more focused on my military interview, which was due next month in Bengaluru. It was a direct interview opportunity I earned because of my good scores in class twelve," Shekhawat unfolded his childhood and teenage memories of school and Meera to Kate.

"She was never in love with you, I guess," Kate concluded.

"No... she never was. She never tried to understand me," Shekhawat added.

"Are you still in touch with her?" Kate asked, sounding sympathetic.

"We're not in touch..." Shekhawat got up from his chair and stretched his arms.

"Military interview! What's that about?" Kate asked.

"It's a five-day interview process for selecting officer candidates into the services," Shekhawat explained.

"Major, your story is really interesting so far," Kate smiled.

"There are many more memories lined up to share, and you're definitely going to enjoy the roller coaster ride through them," Shekhawat said with excitement.

"That's what I'm doing so far," Kate replied.

"Hey, tell me, what was that thing for which your senior punished you when you were in your fourth semester of training?" Kate asked with a mischievous smile.

"Oh... that thing... Well, Kartik and I got caught having fritters in the out classes that took place outside of CTW but still within the main campus of the military college. We were caught by a senior, who, ironically, was also having fritters there," they both laughed heartily.

"So, why did he punish you?" Kate asked, still laughing.

"Because we were seen, and he was the senior," they both laughed even more.

"Kartik and I were famously known as the 'Partners in Crime.' I miss him..." Shekhawat's tone grew more reflective.

"So, you got punished just for having fritters?" Kate asked, intrigued.

"Yes... because having outside food was off-limits for all training cadets," Shekhawat explained.

"This wasn't the only time. We got caught again for having fritters—this time by an officer instructor, and that's when things went really wrong. We received official punishments," Shekhawat laughed, reminiscing.

"And that's still not the end of it. Between the official and unofficial punishments, we barely had time for breakfast or lunch, which forced us to sneak out for fritters again. We were caught once more, this time by a drill instructor responsible for maintaining discipline. That was a record in the whole wing," Shekhawat added with a chuckle.

Kate laughed out loud. "So, your training was all about getting caught and repeating the same blunders?"

"No... In our final term, there was a Titan competition between all four platoons—Alpha, Bravo, Charlie, and Delta. For five terms, we watched our seniors compete, and I always dreamed of competing in my final term like a warrior. We prepared for that competition for four months, and I was cocky about my chances. Being good at physicals and running, I assumed I'd definitely place in the top five. So, I hardly practiced for the event.

Let me tell you, this event involved a 12 km run with a full battle load, followed by an obstacle course with twelve obstacles, and finally, 200 meters of freestyle swimming.

On the day of the event, I started running at a comfortable pace, but soon realized that most of the guys had already passed me. I panicked and, instead of gradually picking up speed, I hastened and nearly ran out of breath after the run. I managed to place in the top five for the 12 km run, but by the time I reached the obstacle course, I was completely drained. I couldn't compete with the top five or anyone else in that competition. Slowly, everyone behind me overtook me, and I ended up among the last five," Shekhawat laughed at the bitter memory.

"Don't tell me you ended up last," Kate laughed too.

"No... no... I finished just before the last guy, who had a knee injury in the previous term. The moment I reached the finish point, my platoon commander walked up to me and said, 'You've disgraced the whole platoon,' and left. He was right—Naresh and Nikhil both placed in the top ten. I did feel bad, but it was all my fault. The best part of the army is that people quickly forget everything with the arrival of the next event, and so was my case. The Titan competition became a day-old memory. Two days later, we had our ball night, and everyone was busy preparing their six bravos, the dinner night rig. In the army, there's a uniform for every special occasion, which is why an army officer's wardrobe is more stuffed than a lady's wardrobe. This was the event we were all desperately waiting for..." Shekhawat smiled broadly.

"...I was dating a girl named Natasha. She was into modeling, and we met through a mutual friend of mine while I was studying at Delhi University," Shekhawat added.

"I still remember... She was wearing a light pink knee-length skirt and looked absolutely gorgeous. She was the tallest among all the girls at the ball night," Shekhawat was lost in the memories.

"I still remember Chandan walking up to me and asking, 'Man... how did you manage to get her?' To which I replied, 'She's my girl, buddy. I didn't manage like Nikhil did.' Shortly after, the MCs made an announcement for the commander and his wife," Shekhawat recalled.

"The first lady, the commander's wife, along with the commander, stood up on the podium and rolled a glittering ball, probably the size of a football, and with that, the night commenced. The DJ started playing songs for the evening... Oh, I forgot to tell you something..."

"...And what's that?" Kate asked.

"Before this, we were all called up on the dais to introduce our ball partners and how we met. Nikhil had managed to secure a date with an air hostess the same day and was gloating about his skills and how proud he was until they were both called up on the dais for the introduction. What happened next gave us a memory to relish for years to come. Nikhil named her wrongly during the introduction, and without a second's hesitation, the lady vanished from there and subsequently from the ball night. It was a hilarious moment for all of us, though not for him. He was thoroughly embarrassed. We laughed so hard—my coursemates made fun of that moment for a long time," Shekhawat said.

As he narrated the event, Kate started laughing.

"How terrible... obviously, any lady would do the same," Kate commented while still laughing.

CHAPTER FIVE

Journey to the forward

"How did you channel your interests after being commissioned?" Kate asked.

"Nothing was planned. Opportunities just presented themselves, and I kept exploring them.

After getting commissioned, I had a year before joining my battalion, so I enrolled in coding classes at an institute outside the base. Luckily, Navas joined me as well. We attended classes every Wednesday and Saturday. But as time passed, the classes became more of a chore, and after three weeks, we decided to quit. I realized then that no one can guide or teach you better than yourself. So, I started learning coding on my own. It was only when I was stationed at the forward posts that I began to understand the challenges the army faced. I combined my passion for coding with those challenges and created what is now known as GRAVITON.

The most important thing is to always equip yourself with multiple tools. And by tools, I mean skills. They always come in handy," Shekhawat replied, his tone brimming with excitement.

"That's enlightening... Major, could you shed some light on your combat experience? Specifically, your time in the forward localities," Kate asked, her smile revealing a mix of curiosity and amusement. By now, she had figured out that she could coax Shekhawat into sharing his story with just a smile.

"Alright then. Here's the story…

Tenga, 30th September. We received orders to move to the Nam Ka Chu valley, a disputed region between India and China, located in NEFA (North East Frontier Agency), Arunachal Pradesh. We were the Alpha Company of the battalion, stationed at Tenga, NEFA.

It was early morning when my batman came rushing to my room, knocking urgently.

'Saab, commander saab is on the line,' he announced, knocking again. As a captain, I didn't expect a call from the commander, especially not at 0400 hours.

I rushed to the office tent, located just a few meters from my room near the Kameng River. Dressed in khaki pants and a white vest, I picked up the radio set, my runner standing by with a diary and pen, ready to take notes as was customary.

'Shekhawat, Commander 9 Infantry Brigade here, based in Tawang. We're planning to move to Rongla by 1st October, and I want you to take your company to the general area Bridge III near the Dhaula post, guarded by the Rajput Battalion. You need to reach Dhaula by the last light on 3rd October. These are direct orders. Your commanding officer will be informed shortly.'

'Roger, sir,' I responded as the commander hung up.

The situation felt strange. It's rare for a captain to receive direct orders from a one-star general, hinting at the seriousness of the situation. I informed the adjutant of my battalion about the conversation and my move plan. The rest of my battalion had already moved to Delhi for a peace posting after spending more than three years in the field.

We were the rear company left behind to hand over the charge to the incoming battalion.

At 0430 hours, the three platoon commanders stood before my worn-out table.

'The orders from the brigade are clear. Prepare for the move by 1000 hours. Any questions? Proceed,' I briefed them.

The platoon commanders left to prepare for the move. Considering the gravity of the situation, I called the telephone exchange at Tezpur, where the Corps headquarters was located.

'A private number for me, Captain Shekhawat calling,' I told the exchange operator, providing my home number.

When my mother answered, her voice still echoes in my ears. 'Hello,' she said, and on hearing my voice, she broke into tears. It hit me hard emotionally.

'Mom, I may not be able to talk for long. Please take care of yourself and dad,' I said as the call ended after a minute.

It was a brief conversation, but it left a lasting memory. With that, I went back to my room, where breakfast was already served.

'Saab ji, today's breakfast is khichdi and milk. The rest of the mess is loaded in the 1-ton truck,' my batman reported.

'Alright, Karnail, go have your breakfast and finish packing,' I replied. Karnail was a 6-foot Khalsa with a stout build. After he left, I had my breakfast and packed my belongings, which wasn't much.

Tenga was pleasant in September and October, but we were clueless about the weather in the forward areas at 16,000 feet above sea level.

After checking on my men, we departed from Tenga by 1000 hours. The valley was stunning, with winding roads through lush green hills. I was in my jeep, enjoying the cool breeze and scenic landscape, unaware of what lay ahead. After two hours, we reached Dirang Dzong, a small town with a few shops, where we had the lunch we had brought along. We left Dirang by 1245 hours, heading for Tawang, where the Brigade headquarters were located, the last point with metalled roads. Beyond that, we had to march on foot.

After an eight-hour drive, we were exhausted when we reached the Brigade HQ at 2000 hours. We were instructed to stay the night and prepare for the forward move. We stayed in a bunker at Tawang, lying on the floor with a few quilts issued by the brigade. I was in a tent. The next day promised to be tough, with a 40 to 45 km trek ahead over gradually rising terrain.

The next morning, Karnail stood outside my tent at 0450 hours.

'Jai Hind Saab, here's your tea,' his voice firm.

'Come in, Karnail,' I invited him in. He placed the glass on the table and began packing my things. I sat down, took the glass, and sipped my tea in the cold Tawang weather. Karnail briefed me, 'Saab ji, we're moving to Lampu at 0530 hours. Everything's ready.'

I enjoyed the morning tea as fog enveloped the surroundings, obscuring the hills. There was no network, so I relied on an mp3 player that also played the radio. Mohammad Rafi and Lata Mangeshkar's songs filled the air until the news broke in:

'Urgent announcement from the Ministry of Defence: Tensions between China and India have escalated over the border dispute. All leaves for soldiers and officers have been canceled, and immediate deployment orders have been issued.'

This didn't surprise me, but I hadn't expected tensions with China to escalate so quickly. Karnail soon returned.

'Saab ji, packing's done, and your dress is ready,' he reported before marching off.

I was used to hearing the term "packing" during moves, and I was tired of it. I got dressed, polished my boots, which added a touch of authority to my uniform, and headed to the high ground a few meters from my tent where my company was assembled. Upon arrival, Karnail took my bag, and my senior JCO gave me the company's report. We then set off toward our destination, unaware of our specific role at the historic Dhaula post. We were told to make contact with the 12 Rajput Battalion and that I was to report to its commanding officer. The foot track wound through the valley and hills, so we moved in line formation, with me leading the first platoon and the others following.

After four hours of marching, we reached Gokthang by 1000 hours, where we saw locals with their yaks. We took a 15-minute breakfast break. The langar staff prepared hot tea for us, which was a godsend in the cold weather. There was fog all around, and my men were shivering as we lacked proper winter clothing. The only way to stay warm was to keep moving.

After the break, we resumed our march. Some soldiers chatted while others hummed the latest songs. We weren't thinking about the impending conflict. It felt like just another routine exercise. We marched on, reaching Lumpo village at 1400 hours, where we crossed a log bridge and headed for Dhaula. By evening, we were exhausted when we finally reached Neliya, just a few more hours from our destination.

We took a 10-minute break at Neliya. To our surprise, a few locals came toward us and served us hot tea. Their hospitality was a relief and an energy boost for my men. We thanked them before continuing. Finally, at 2100 hours, we reached the Dhaula post, guarded by the Rajput Battalion. We were stopped at the sentry post.

'Jai Hind Saab, are you from the 30 Punjab Battalion?' the soldier asked, to which my senior JCO nodded. He escorted the men to the barracks, and I was taken to the CO's office.

'Jai Hind, Sir,' I greeted the Rajput Battalion's CO.

'Welcome to Dhaula, Shekhawat,' he responded warmly. He gestured for me to sit as he briefed me on my area of responsibility and informed me where my company would be stationed.

'Shekhawat, you and your company will be stationed at Point 4690, about 10 to 12 kilometers from here. You'll be assisting Captain Kartik and his platoon there.'

The name sounded familiar. The CO further explained the battalion's area of responsibility and our duties.

'Stay here tonight and move to Point 4690 before first light tomorrow,' he added. That night, we rested at Dhaula, where we could see the heavy developments across the Nam Ka Chu river. It was clear that China had been preparing for a long time. We saw well-constructed roads across the river, over the Thag La ridge. The next morning, we began our move to Point 4690 at 0400 hours.

That was our last peaceful night before the storm hit."

… the loss

Point 4690

10 October

We could see the Chinese built up along the river. Preparations on our side were minimal as compared to what China has done. Kartik was standing on the view point made up of shacks by our guys to see the other side. He was lost in his thoughts. I called out him and kept my hand over his shoulder.
'What happened? you seem lost today. Is everything Ok?'
'Yashvardhan, I have a year-old daughter without a mother. She is all I have now. Her Grandmother, my mother, back at home is her only stand. I am just worried if something happened to me here, who will take care of her. I want to see my daughter growing up. I know these thoughts doesn't suit you when you have the men waiting for your orders', he was calm, I never saw him like that. I too realised that we are turning old now. I turned back and went to the shack we were sharing…", Shekhawat was interrupted by Kate.
"Sorry Major, Is this the same guy you started your journey with, boarded the bus to the officers' training academy, getting caught for having fritters in the military college?", Kate tried to draw some conclusion.
"Yes, the very same guy I told you about", Shekhawat clarified.
"The next day Kartik was told to carry out patrolling in the DMZ, demilitarised zone. That morning was the last

time I have seen him.

0000 hrs (Indian time) and 0230 hrs (Chinese time) the aggressive patrol of PLA was seen near the Indian tower with latest assault rifles. The OP (Observation Post) informed the base regarding this. It was an unexpected move, since the Chinese diplomats the previous day made it clear over the hotline that there will be a routine PLA patrol but it was an aggressive patrol, which they generally carry out once a year.

A QRT (Quick Reaction Team) was called and Kartik was immediately sent to the tower region. Stone shower came over head of Indian soldiers as they were trying to climb up from the Rear side of the tower. Kartik observed that the tower has already been captured by the Chinese aggressive patrol. Stones, because strict cease fire is being observed at LAC (Line of Actual Control), so there is a mutual understanding between both the sides that none will open fire unless the order comes up from top-brass. 'SPREADDDD……. All of you take your positions, lie down and wait for my further orders', Kartik, without wasting a breath ordered the soldiers to take cover in the available vegetation.

The communication guy was besides Kartik.

'Alpha 1 for Tiger message over', Kartik made an initial contact with the commanding officer over the radio set.

'Tiger… OK. Over', Kartik heard a voice over his radio set.

'Tiger, Tower down. Over', Kartik informed the CO regarding the present condition of the tower region. (Heavy fire from the Chinese side was experienced by the Indian side)

'wait for further instructions. Over', replied the commanding officer. (Don't go up and wait for further instructions)
'Roger over'.

The communication trailed off. The base tried contacting Kartik but failed to establish any radio contact with the quick reaction team headed by Kartik.
Tiger kept contacting but no reply from the other side came. Soon, we were sent for the back-up and after an hour or so we reached near the tower region. We were ambushed. It was a bait. I got hit by a bullet in one of my shoulders. We retaliated them back but they were having a numerical superiority over us. Our whole back-up team was ambushed and only two of us, me and my radio operator, survived the incident. For two days our bodies were covered under snow and were fortunate enough to be discovered by the recovery team sent by the commanding officer Rajput Battalion. It was an aggressive PLA patrol that cordoned us and inflicted heavy casualties upon us. We didn't have any technology there, so we were not able to prove and project this mishap at an international level and by the time I came into senses in the military hospital, I came to know that Kartik was KIA (Killed-In Action)", with a trembling voice Shekhawat stopped.

"Are you alright Major?", Kate asked in a concerned tone.

"Yes... yes I am fine", Shekhawat tried to control his emotions.

She held his hand in hers and lightly hugged him.

"That's alright Major. You miss him?", Kate asked

"I miss him... a lot", Shekhawat replied with wet eyes.

"Vani was hardly a year old when her grandmother, Kartik's mother too expired. Now, it became my moral obligation to take care of her", Shekhawat added.

"She knows about all this?", Kate asked.

"no... All she knows is that I am her father and that is what she should know...", in a very firm voice Shekhawat answered.

"wait here Kate... I will be back in a minute", Shekhawat whisked inside and after a minute or so brought a diary along.

He handed over the diary to her, with a bookmark.

"This is regarding...", Kate gazed at him in oblivion.

"This is the poem that I framed for Kartik", Shekhawat confronted.

Tall trees, beautiful valleys with its green,
Made the early morning scene.

Nam Ka Chu in between both lands,
Men across guarding with guns in hands.

So was the place I had been,
Men ready to sacrifice with motivation keen.

Along with men, away from home,
Long was the time I last shown.

One fine day, the red flag crossed the river,
Men along retaliated till they shiver.

Rounds were over and magazines were empty by one,
War was fought with bare hands by men.

Waves over waves attacked the handful,
Handful crushed the waves to the full.

Wounded I was, as I stabbed the one in chest,
Lied peacefully, with a relief as I did my best.

"That is an emotional piece major... I am sorry for your loss...", Kate exclaimed in a sympathetic tone.

"That' alright Kate...", Shekhawat replied.

CHAPTER SIX

Start-ups

"That is an emotional piece major... I am sorry for your loss...", Kate exclaimed in a sympathetic tone.

"That' alright Kate...", Shekhawat replied.

To divert his emotions, Kate immediately changed the topic.

"How was the shift outside military?" Kate enquired.

"Painful initially, but I got used to it with the passage of time," Shekhawat replied, recalling the old times.

"So, what was your first venture, Major?" Kate asked curiously, a gentle smile on her face.

"Green Energy," Shekhawat replied abruptly.

"Specifically?" Kate asked, slightly confused.

"BioGas. On returning to my hometown, I realized that the villagers had enough cattle to support a biogas and green energy project. I gathered myself and started working on it. It was a simple setup that required less investment compared to my other ventures, and the best part was it was eco-friendly," Shekhawat explained.

"I see. Can you narrate it? How did you start, and what problems did you encounter while making it fully functional and available for public use?"

"The aim was clear: to generate and distribute green energy at much cheaper rates than the state's electricity department. At that time, it was Rs. 6 per unit, and I provided electricity at Rs. 2 per unit. The villagers liked the project since it saved them a lot of money. Initially, my own family was against the idea, as it seemed like a failed project. In many places in our country, people were executing this idea on a much smaller scale with not much encouraging results," Shekhawat narrated.

"And how was yours different?" Kate asked, amused.

"It was on similar lines but on a bigger scale. I catered my green energy to around ten villages, comprising an average of fifty homes each," Shekhawat added.

"So you must be earning well from this project?" Kate asked in an amused tone.

"I would say satisfactory earnings. But I was happier to see that my firm was getting popular amongst the locals. It earned me and my family a huge respect. My earnings from this project were around Rs. 5 lakhs per month, which was enough for us."

"I got motivated to invest more in the green energy sector and found a way to create more renewable energy assets for the people. We started outsourcing solar panels and vertical axis wind turbine generators in bulk. The best part of these wind turbines was their smaller size and affordable price," Shekhawat explained.

"So you diversified your field by adding new ideas to generate electricity," Kate remarked, gazing at him with curiosity.

"Yes, we did. Biogas required a lot of biodegradable waste and consumed a lot of manpower. Initially, we earned good profits, but eventually, the graph went down. There came a time when I was left with just a million bucks. I had to decide whether to let my company die slowly or take a risk and invest in other renewable energy sources," he said, an old worry appearing on his face as he clasped his hands and sighed deeply.

"And to our surprise, the market for renewable energy boomed and overtook our biogas sector within two years. In the following years, more than twenty villages and five towns joined the mission, which forced us to establish customer care services and local offices in nearly all the villages and towns that became our clients," he said, a proud, determined shine on his face that Kate could sense.

"What about the biogas plant? Did you abandon it?" Kate asked curiously.

"No, it's still functional and provides free electricity to everyone who supplies the plant with biodegradable waste. Mostly, the villagers from the nearby area benefit from it."

"That's really amazing, Major. It's impressive that you're in a business that's making profits and winning the hearts of the people," Kate said, smiling and giving him a light pat on the shoulder.

Shekhawat reciprocated with a gentle smile while holding his coffee mug. Meanwhile, dusk turned into a beautiful evening, and the view of the landscape became even more scenic.

It was 6 PM and dusk was turning to a darker night with a continuous snowfall outside. Ramveer walked up to them in the porch.

"*Saab ji fireplace ready hai*", Ramveer lit the fire in the fireplace and informed Shekhawat regarding the same.

"Kate... wanna join inside?", Shekhawat asked as he stood up.

"Only if you promise to resume...", Kate smiled and got up too.

"That is what I am doing since morning", both of them chuckled.

Ramveer cleared the porch and took away the empty coffee mugs to the kitchen. Shekhawat and Kate went inside the villa towards the fireplace room.

Just in front of the fireplace there were two sofa chairs placed. Both of them sat on them and continued their conversation.

"Tell me more of Meera", Kate sat crossed legs, one over the other.

"What do you want to know about her?", Shekhawat asked.

"Like... Didn't you see her after school ever. Like face to face", Kate asked curiously.

"I did... many a times...", Shekhawat replied.

"How about wine?... Wanna have one?", Shekhawat immediately changed the topic.

"Yeah... anything", Kate replied.

"*Ramveer wine leke aao... Chambertin...*", Shekhawat shouted out to Ramveer.

Next few minutes there was a complete silence. All four eyes were gazing at the fire when suddenly Ramveer broke the ice. Ramveer showed up with a bottle of wine and glasses over a wooden tray.

"When was the last time you talked to her?", Kate asked.

"a year back... I guess...", Shekhawat sipped the wine from the glass meanwhile.

"So, how was the interaction like?", Kate asked curiously with a strange happiness. A nostalgia casted over him.

"It was normal...nothing very special... How about if I tell you my first interaction with her after school days. You will definitely gonna enjoy listening to it", Shekhawat wanted to uncover his side from the very beginning.

"...whatever way you like major... it is your story, so obviously you can narrate it the way you want...", Kate shrugged her shoulders while keeping the glass over the knee length wooden peg table placed between both the chairs.

The song was being played in the background, snowfall outside and fire being lit in the dark room comprising of Kate and Shekhawat. It was a beautiful ambience and definitely Kate was enjoying it.

"You know what Major, coming here... all the way from California is now I feel a huge blessing for me... I never enjoyed someone's company this way ever before in my life in the states", Kate expressed her happiness to Shekhawat.

"I am glad to hear this... Pleasure is all mine Kate", Shekhawat replied. Shekhawat held his glass back, sipped and resumed his story.

"So, I was newly commissioned and there was a party at the military college. We were officers now and no more cadets, so we had more time now with us and no watchdogs over us. It was the month of november and more than hundred officers, including many senior officers posted at the military college, were gathered along with their wives and children, some bachelors with their girls excluding me and Kartik who were standing beside the pool and were having our beer when I caught Meera's sight for the first time after so long in that party. We were young lieutenants. I saw her with a Captain of probably three to four years of service. This time it was she, who walked up to me. She was wearing a pink knee length skirt and a black jacket. As usual she was looking gracious.

'Hey Yashvardhan... How are you? Been a long-time man...', Meera came near to me and there was a strange smile over her face. I was stunned that how come she recognised me. She was not the Meera I knew. I thought that she will try to avoid me the moment she will see me.

'Sorry ma'am... I didn't recognise you...', these were the words to her from my side, soon after which I walked away from the spot with Kartik following me.

'Shekhawat who was that lady? Do you know her? Man... she was looking gorgeous?', Kartik asked me regarding Meera. I was quiet for a while but I told him finally about Meera.

'She was a classmate. We studied together in school', I told him about Meera. He further asked me that why I avoided her. To which I replied that I had a bad past with her which I don't want to remember anymore. Hearing this, Kartik killed his curiosity of knowing her further.

Soon after few moments we saw from far that her alleged boyfriend from the bar counter walked up to her and both of them left the party...", Shekhawat told Kate about his initial encounter with Meera after being commissioned.

"So, this was the same boyfriend she talked to you about over the phone?", Kate asked Shekhawat referring to their previous conversation.

"I don't know...may be... may be not... it hardly bothered me that time", Shekhawat shrugged his shoulders.

"But why you said that you didn't know her", Kate added.

"I don't know... I felt that way... I had no liking left for her... no doubt she was beautiful and I always liked her but, trust me, I didn't want to fall in the loop of talking to her and liking her once again and finally ending up feeling humiliated and bad. So, I thought it's better to avoid her. Although I was a bit rude but I liked it...", Shekhawat chuckled and winked.

"Oh... that's so rude of you", Kate laughed.
Shekhawat got up and inserted the disc into the turntable. It was a melodious song, with room being dark and partially lighted by the fireplace. Kate was looking at Shekhawat.

"Would you mind a dance, Kate?" Shekhawat asked.

"Sure, Major," Kate smiled.

Kate rose and approached the table where a turntable was placed, with Shekhawat standing nearby. He took her hand and placed his other hand on her waist. She, in turn, rested her hand on his shoulder while placing her other hand in his left hand. Both exchanged light smiles, their faces mostly hidden in the darkness, only glimpses visible to each other.

"So, you dance as well," Kate remarked with a smile.

"I told you, ball nights are commonplace in military college," Shekhawat winked. The music and night progressed slowly, shifting the mood suddenly. Kate was no longer concerned about the story; it was a moment they both relished.

A while later, Kate rested her head on Shekhawat's chest, both lost in each other. The dance concluded with the song, and they returned to their seats.

"Sometimes, being with someone whose vibes match yours is amazing. I was lost... lost in the music... Honestly, Major, I enjoyed your company," Kate expressed her happiness to Shekhawat.

"Likewise," Shekhawat replied.

"So, are you married?" Shekhawat inquired, a question Kate anticipated.

"No, I'm not married... nor dating anyone," Kate replied instantly, as if expecting the question.

"Though I've dated quite a few guys... work kept me busy, and those dates never lasted morc than a week," they both chuckled.

It was 8:00 PM, and Ramveer sought permission to close the fireplace.

"The dinner is ready, Saab ji," the butler informed Shekhawat, and moments later, they headed to the adjacent dining room.

"Major, were you working on anything while you were in the army, or did your interests shift suddenly?" Kate asked, her curiosity evident.

"I was expecting that question, Kate," Shekhawat chuckled.

"Well, I worked on several projects while in the army. My first project was a smart mine—a mine that deactivates itself if someone accidentally steps on it and says a specific command," Shekhawat explained.

"That's a life-saving innovation, Major. Very clever of you," Kate said, clearly impressed by his ingenuity.

"So, was the project funded by the Army?" Kate inquired, intrigued.

"No, I worked on it independently. I did show it to my superiors, but they rejected the project, saying it lacked a professional touch. I had to abandon it," Shekhawat admitted, his tone tinged with disappointment.

"After that, I started working on No Network Mobile Service (NNMS). What happened to one of my course mates on the LAC motivated me to develop it," Shekhawat added.

"What is NNMS?" Kate asked, her tone polite.

"It's a specialized communication system that allows mobile communication within military zones without relying on traditional network towers. It's secure and enables data sharing, chatting, and even calling family using relay stations placed every ten kilometers," Shekhawat elaborated.

"That sounds amazing," Kate said, genuinely impressed.

"People like you are rare," she complimented him with a smile.

As they finished dinner, Shekhawat asked, "Would you mind taking a walk outside, Kate? It's something I do often after dinner."

"Alright," Kate nodded in agreement.

… the walk

The snowfall had stopped, revealing a clear sky adorned with glittering stars, casting a serene beauty over the landscape. A fountain in the garden in front of the villa's façade trickled softly, adding to the peaceful atmosphere. The cold air carried the scent of winter, with trees and shrubs blanketed in a thick layer of snow that shimmered in the moonlight, giving the garden a magical, almost otherworldly charm.

"It's mesmerizing. This landscape feels heavenly. It's giving me Christmas and New Year vibes…" Kate said, her voice filled with a strange happiness.

"It reminds me of my childhood when my dad would dress up as Santa and bring me gifts… Every year, I'd wait so eagerly for Christmas Eve, followed by New Year's Eve… It was all so wonderful…" The nostalgic setting brought back warm memories for Kate.

"That's why I love living in the hills… It brings a sense of peace. It's like you're in conversation with nature, enjoying its beauty. And by the way, it's less than a week until the New Year," Shekhawat said, sharing his thoughts while subtly reminding Kate of the upcoming festivities.

As they walked along the garden path, Shekhawat couldn't help but admire Kate's beauty.

"Hey, didn't you ever fall in love with anyone after Meera?" Kate asked softly.

"I'm falling for someone... right now..." Shekhawat whispered, his cheeks flushing.

"Say that again... I didn't quite catch it..." Kate turned towards him, a playful smile dancing on her lips. It was a moment neither of them had anticipated.

In a moment of weakness—or perhaps fate—Shekhawat moved closer to her. This time, Kate didn't resist. Instead, she leaned into the moment. They could feel each other's warm breath on their lips. Shekhawat gently tucked her hair behind her ear with one hand, while his other hand rested on her waist, his touch sending tremors through Kate. Kate, her hands on his shoulder and chest, drew closer, her eyes locked onto his with a faint smile.

Slowly, Shekhawat pressed his lips to hers in a gentle, smooth kiss. The kiss deepened, lingering for several minutes as they stood in the moonlit garden.

It was an unexpected moment, and the saying—"the unexpected happens at the most unexpected times"—came vividly to life for them.

After walking a few more yards, they found an easy bench in the garden and sat down, Shekhawat still holding her hand.

"I've never felt so free, so alive…" Kate said, her happiness mirrored in Shekhawat's expression.

"I'm glad you're here. Would you like to see my laboratory?" Shekhawat offered.

"Really? That would be so cool! I'd love to see your work," Kate replied, her excitement palpable.

The night was perfect for both of them. Soon after, they headed inside the villa. As they reached the main entrance, Kate spoke up.

"How about we talk more about you?" she asked suddenly.

"Sure… Another walk?" Shekhawat suggested.

"No, it's getting cold outside. Let's walk to my room," Kate proposed.

"Okay," Shekhawat agreed.

They made their way to Kate's room, located to the left of the main entrance. The room was dimly lit, bathed in the soft glow of a bedside lamp. As Shekhawat pushed the door open and stepped inside, Kate moved closer to him. Their eyes locked in an intense gaze, and without a word, Kate guided Shekhawat's hand to the back of her head, lightly pulling him toward her.

Shekhawat responded, wrapping his arms around her waist. Kate cupped his jawline with one hand and gave him a soft peck on the lips. They stood there, eyes transfixed on each other, still holding on tightly.

In a seductive whisper, Kate leaned in close to his ear, "Yash... Don't let it go"

Their lovemaking continued for an hour or so.

Afterward, as they lay together in the soft glow of the room, Kate's eyes wandered to a photograph on the bedside table. She reached out, picking it up with a curious smile.

"Is that you when you were a child?" she asked, her tone light and affectionate.

Shekhawat nodded, a smile tugging at the corners of his lips.

"You were cute," Kate remarked, still smiling as she placed the photo back.

"Tell me something about your childhood," she added, her curiosity piqued.

... childhood memories

"Ok... I do remember that we used to live in a village in Himachal Pradesh. One fine day, I was sitting beneath a maple tree and was quietly watching my mother gathering firewood. It was 2002 and I was admitted to 1st grade of AJAY NEW MODEL PUBLIC SCHOOL, which was probably the only English medium school of the area, covering one of the twenty villages of Hamirpur district, Himachal Pradesh. My father was serving in the Army and most of the times he was on the front, serving the mother land. Me, my poor mother and my innocent sister was all I had that time. Those days the salary of government employees, especially soldiers were minimal. My father was in Kashmir that time and the environment like today was not very friendly there.

'Mom, till what time should we be leaving for home?' I asked my mother very hopefully.

It was bright noon of autumn and I was starving like a rat, sitting under the shady maple tree. This was my favourite tree. Over the years we had developed a close association with each other, as most of my days in vacations and school after hours were spent with him. Everyday my mother used to carry an old rice sack, which she used to lay out for me like a mat under that tree and over which I used to sit and talk to the tree for hours and hours. 'Yashu, beta wait, let me gather firewood for your dinner'. My mom was very thin and the stress over her made her look pale like a woman in early forties, though she was hardly thirty years of age. Our home was located in a village called *Bada Gaon*, to wit, it was not a very big village. We used to live in a mud house with an old lady, who pretended to be my grandma, which actually she was not. She was a cousin of my grandpa from far. She used to torture my mother like hell, used to beat my sister for being a girl. There was a corner besides the stairs to the upper small place where she used to keep all her sticks and whenever I used to come down from the upper small place, I used to stare at them in fear. There was a phobia that developed in me from those sticks and took a toll over my head for many years.

After waiting for few more minutes my mom came to me with a dupatta tied to her head, this was the regular image of her in my mind for many upcoming years. 'Let's go Yashu'. I folded the mat, jumped in joy, held her fingers with my little hands, that were probably too soft for those torn-skinned fingers. On the way, while going back to home from the woods, there was a place where she used to go, sit for ten minutes and then we used to continue our home journey after that. It was her regular practice. As the days passed, one day I went to her and saw her weeping. I held her shoulder with my hand.

'Mom what happened why are you crying?'

That was too sweet of me to ask her and she looked at me and hugged me tightly. Every day she used to weep for ten-minutes, this was probably my first discovery cum encounter of my mother's strong heart.

'When will I get out of this hell? When will we get rid of that old lady? When your dad will come to see us? ….'

There were many questions that piled over my grey and I could not figure out any correct answer to those. She quietly got up, held my hand took me to our mud shack which used to drip during heavy rains. Luckily it was the month of summers. We had a small black and white television. Those days me and my sister used to desperately wait for Sundays. Sundays were happening because 'SHAKTIMAN' and many animated series were played on DD National, the only channel that our cycle rim antenna could deliver us. Those days India was not very developed, especially rural India. My sister never accompanied my mother to the woods. She had her own girl gang in the village with whom she used to play all day long and sometimes had lunch at any one of the gang member's home. She was a real chubby kid. The only thing I hated about her the most was though she was in third standard she was habitual of keeping her thumb inside her mouth and I used to scold her many times for doing that and many a times we used to fight, although only two years elder to me, she used to treat me like her own child. This was our regular schedule during the summer vacations.

I still remember that afternoon when the news broke out regarding Operation Parakram, led by the Indian side against the Pakistan. My father's battalion was first in line with the enemy in the western front. As soon as, I reached home I saw my mother sitting over the floor near the window and sobbing. She was holding a letter in her hand.

By that time, I got familiar with the army envelopes and I, without a single prick of mistake, understood very well that it was from my dad. I politely asked my mother what happened? Why she was crying?
'The war will start soon. Your dad has gone to Rajasthan. If he will be alive, he will come next year to see us'.

All I could gather was that he was coming successive year to see us. After some time for no reason, I saw my mother making a stamp with a sketch pen over the white envelope, inside which she kept her heart, which she wanted my father to read. It seemed a bit wonky to me, as prior to this I never saw any self-made stamp. She used to send me to the shop to purchase one whenever she wanted to write a letter to my dad. After preparing lunch for me, she took me along with her to the post office, where she was about to slip the letter inside the red box.
'Madam wait, this is not acceptable, you cannot make stamp with your hands', The post master stopped her.

'There was no stamp in the shop. So, I made one with my hands as it is an urgent piece and I need to deliver it as soon as possible'.
'Ma'am it is not in my hands, the head office will not accept it and your letter will get lost. It is for your benefit I am saying'. The post master took out a stamp from his pocket and handed it over to mom. She glued it tightly over the envelope and posted the letter.
'Thank you bhaisahab (brother)', there was a light smile of accomplishment over her face. I used to see my father twice a year and that year he didn't even appear for once.

We had a small field in the village and a goat which used to provide us with milk. Although my mother used to milk her in the evening, but that old lady never let us have a single drop of it. Our condition was way pathetic. Very rarely mom used to give us one-rupee coin, which I used to assume as a big amount. It was given to my sister, as she was the eldest and was asked to share with me. In the lunch break at school, I used to go running from my class to her so as to make sure she doesn't spend whole without me. We were really very tender.

Whenever the old lady tried to frighten me with stick, I used to warn her my father is in army and he will beat her if she threatens us anymore. She used to mock me by saying— I am afraid of you now as your father will bring whole army here to beat me. There was a late-night holy day (jaagaran) in the winters and me along with my sister and mom had gone to attend it and the old lady remained at home. We came late home from the function. The old lady was waiting with her stick in-ready position in one of her hands and as soon we entered, a sharp shout of abuse strike all three of us. She started beating my mother and my sister, calling both of them characterless. I was stunned that day and could not decipher the whole situation. My mother went upstairs to our small space and started sobbing, hugging me and my sister. My sister too was crying in her arms clasped around her and I was afraid. The next day mom went to serve breakfast to that old lady. As soon as she handed over the brass plate with bowls over it to her, she frowned at her and in the next instant she threw it in the air which strike the wall ahead and all of curd, dals were covering the floor. 'Bitch I don't eat animal's food', these words still echo my ears whenever I remember this incident and even right now, when I am telling you this. Mom used to write this to my father. He too was helpless as he was in the front and we had no other home to stay. Literally we were helpless and clueless as what to do'.

There was one more in our gang. His name was Anku. Anku comparatively belonged to a rich family and in the whole village only they had a coloured television. On Sundays we used to go to his home and our whole gang used to watch television. Aunty was a very kind lady. She used to prepare lunch for our whole gang. We all loved her. One thing, upon which I always argued with Anku was that "my shaktiman" (black shaktiman) was better than the one wearing dark red costume (his shaktiman). I was completely unaware of the fact that it was due to the fact that we were having a black and white TV that my shaktiman had to wear a black costume. I was very naïve. The months rolled by and finally in our village one of the families from '*gabli saatthh*' (middle village area) village took a landline connection. It was a big relief for my mother. This was probably the first telephone service for our village. I can never forget the black glossy colour of that chat box. Now, every Sunday my dad used to call my mother at sharp 1000 hrs and me and my mother used to eagerly wait at their home, waiting for a single bell to ring. The situation which I could never decipher at that time was that I used to see my mother very happy in the morning time and in the evening time very sad. I could not figure out what happens to her after talking to dad. Many a times I thought that it may be because dad scolds her over the line, until that very final day when I too got the chance to say hello to my dad. One fine Sunday morning it so happened that my mother was really depressed and it appeared as if she was up to her brims to convey something important to my dad. The bell rang and my mom picked up. The first thing she said was- ' *Ahaan no ethi te laiyawa……*' (Take us with u). That was the first time I came along with her inside the telephone room. Watching this condition of my mom, although I didn't understand anything, I too started crying and my dad heard my crying. He wanted to talk to me. I held the phone and said- '*daddy g dadi ahaan jo dande maardi, kane gaaliyan kad di, je tuhan ni aana ta main telephona bich hi badi ne aai yana tuhan kol*' (Dad the old lady beats us and abuses us, if you won't come then I will come to you through telephone). This had a deep impact on him. He informed the whole matter to his company commander and that time his battalion was posted at Hissar Cantt. Luckily, we got the army accommodation. He reached us in the summers of 2003.Our escape from that hamlet was a very interesting and story. The old lady had gone to visit her daughter. Dad came home. That night we had our dinner and as usual we all were on that single bed. Let me tell you it was not a king size bed. It was a '*manja*' (single small bed). I was completely unaware of the impact that my words had made on my dad. Me and my sister were unaware of the fact that this night will be our last night at bada gaon. The next morning mom woke us up, me and my sister, at 0500 hrs. It was winters and was still dark outside. As we came down after washing our faces, we saw dad and mom was packing in hurry. I asked mom what happened. She didn't reply anything and was busy packing. The next moment I remember me and my sister were wearing our outing rigs. I was wearing a blue trouser, which was little tight for my waist and a check shirt. My sister was wearing a dark brown trouser and a similar check shirt. The plan was to escape the village before anyone could see us, try to stop us or late us. At sharp 0600 hrs we all four were standing in the waiting area of the 'Thala' market. The shops were still closed. There was a pin drop silence, which was later broken by an incoming '*sarkari bus*' (Himachal Roadways bus). As my mom and dad saw the bus approaching, they hurriedly picked up a suitcase, a carton full of our clothing and another small suitcase. Dad waved his hand in front of the approaching bus, the bus stopped. Dad opened the door, stepped inside and mom firstly passing all the luggage to him and later us and finally climbed up. I was still asking my mom regarding our final destination. For a moment I felt that we are going to my maternal grandma's home.

This thought made me happy till the time my sister interfered and informed me they are going somewhere else. She too was too small to answer my question. The bus reached a place called 'Mehre' (This was where my cousins used to live). I thought maybe we are going to them, but again I was wrong. My dad had only 500 rupees in his pocket. He bought us four apples. We had those apples. Somehow, I don't know how and why I never liked apples. Still, I had that one, since I haven't had anything since morning.

The next thing I remember is I was sitting next to the window and it was evening time, we were still travelling. I was bored and hungry. Sister and me were sitting quietly gaping out of the window and were lost in our own thoughts. We reached the TCP no. 1 gate of Hissar Cantt. It was beautifully decorated with lights, a fountain at the side and two soldiers were guarding the gate with INSAS rifles. For the first time I have seen such an environment. All three of us were mesmerised to see this beautiful landscape. Mom looked at us and said— 'beta this is Hissar Cantt, we will be living inside'. A white Tata Sumo stopped in front of us and we all stepped inside to reach our final destination and that was the army ORs (Other Ranks) accommodation. Our quarter number was 22. It was located on the first floor. We reached at 2000 hrs and first night me and my sister spent at our neighbour's home. Dad and mom were busy shifting and cleaning the new quarter. Me and my sister altogether were lost in such a big city we have no idea about. Before being finally admitted to Army Public School Hissar Cantt, my mother made sure that we do well in the entrance. I still remember, every night I used to draw a hut, a tree, fruits, numbers and alphabets on white sheets. I had no idea that me and my sister were preparing for the entrance examination. Somehow, we cleared it and got admitted into the school. I don't know why but I never liked going school, like many other kids of my age at that time. Many a times I pretended to be indisposed and missed school. Out of all I hated the early morning gatherings for the prayer at school's ground. This school was grand as compared to my previous school. It's play ground was of my previous school's size. I started missing my village and my friends".

There was a pause for few seconds and the void was filled by Kate.

"This really sounds tough Major. Must say you had a tough childhood", Kate exclaimed.

"Yeah ups and downs... It's with everyone. I am no different case. The only difference is how one should groom himself in such conditions", it was a thoughtful statement by Shekhawat.

"True... I agree with that", Kate nodded.

CHAPTER SEVEN

The Lab

"Kate, how familiar are you with science?" Shekhawat asked as they walked down the aisle towards his laboratory, located in the basement of the villa.

"I'm okay with science... I understand some of it," Kate replied.

"Do you know anything about binary?" Shekhawat queried.

"Zeros and ones, I believe... am I right?" Kate responded.

"Correct. Do you know how it works?" Shekhawat continued curiously.

"No, that's about all I know," Kate shrugged.

"Here's the gist: Zeros represent a lower voltage, while ones represent a higher voltage. If the voltage value is below an average threshold, it registers as zero; if above, it's one," Shekhawat explained.

"Alright, that sounds interesting," Kate exclaimed.

"Furthermore, these zeros and ones form the basis of logic, essential in machine code—the fundamental language of microcontrollers, personal computers, and other technologies," Shekhawat added.

"Quite profound," Kate pondered over the information.

"Yes, and that's just the beginning. Have you heard of programming languages like C, C++, Java, Ruby, Kotlin, R, and Python?" Shekhawat asked.

"Yes, I recognize those names. They're used for creating software, right?" Kate replied promptly.

"Exactly. When you write software or applications, their source code is compiled into machine code, which is then executed based on the instructions provided," Shekhawat led her to his latest invention at the heart of the basement. They stood before a bed-shaped machine in the center of the laboratory.

"So, ultimately, it's these zeros and ones that enable all the amazing digital technology," Shekhawat concluded.

"What's your point?" Kate asked, somewhat confused.

"Instead of just using two discrete values—zeros and ones—I've developed a four-value logic system," Shekhawat smiled knowingly.

"Does that mean more precision?" Kate ventured to understand.

"Yes, but I've taken it a step further. I've modeled it after the four base pairs found in DNA—A-T and C-G," Shekhawat explained.

"Wait, let me wrap my head around this. So, what you're saying is incredible, but honestly, it's a bit too much for me to grasp. When I said I'm 'okay' with science, I meant just that, Major," Kate burst out laughing, and Shekhawat joined in.

Shekhawat gestured with both hands, "Alright, Kate... layman's terms..."

"Yeah, please, help me understand," Kate continued to laugh.

"You don't really want to know, right?" Shekhawat asked with a hint of disappointment.

"No, no, go ahead, I really want to understand... seriously. It's just a lot of science," Kate replied, pretending to be serious.

"We have A-T and C-G base pairs in our DNA's double helix. These pairs—Adenine, Thymine, Cytosine, and Guanine—are responsible for carrying genetic information from one generation to the next. Each cell in our body has a unique code for these base pairs, explaining why different body parts have different functions," Shekhawat tried to clarify.

"Don't tell me you're going to start coding humans next?" Kate half-joked, half-serious.

"Exactly," Shekhawat stated proudly.

"Wow, that's mind-boggling! You're crazy... that's so... out of the box," Kate was shocked and surprised.

"It's nearly completed... just around one percent of it is left," Shekhawat informed her.

There was a test mouse. Shekhawat injected it, rendering it unconscious, then amputated its right leg.

"Are you insane? That's not right... you're crazy," Kate was appalled by what she saw.

"Relax, give it a moment. Everything will be fine," Shekhawat reassured her, holding the mouse and placing it on the bed, where he connected it to a needle-shaped device. Then, he moved to the computer behind them and started coding.

Kate was stunned by what she witnessed next.

"Oh my god... that's revolutionary! You're amazing," Kate exclaimed joyfully as she saw the mouse's right leg begin to regenerate.

"I told you everything would be fine... I told you," Shekhawat smiled as he stood up and walked over to her.

Impressed by the technology she had just witnessed, Kate listened as Shekhawat explained the process in simpler terms. For her, seeing was believing, and that was enough.

Dusk fell upon the noon, and as the sun set, they stepped out of his laboratory.

"Kate, let me show you the suburbs of Shimla," Shekhawat suddenly suggested.

"There's nothing out in the suburbs," Kate mocked.

"Oh, but there is... my favorite spot," Shekhawat replied enthusiastically.

"Alright, what's that? A zoo where you find your test subjects!" Kate teased.

"A café... amazing coffee. You'll love it, Kate. And that was Dicy, my pet, not a test subject," Shekhawat clarified, ignoring her sarcasm.

"Hmm... okay, let's see how good it is," Kate agreed.

Shekhawat revved the engine and stopped right in front of the café, located a few miles from the villa.

... café

The café was nestled in snow, its big glass windows emitting colorful lights. It stood alone, with no other shops or civilization nearby—a relic from the British era with a touch of modernity inside.

The café owner, spotting Shekhawat through the window, walked outside and greeted them both with a warm gesture and a welcoming smile.

They sat inside a coffee shop nestled in the quiet suburbs of Shimla.

"Is it always this deserted? I mean, there's no one around," Kate remarked, surprised by the lack of customers except for the guy at the billing counter.

"Very few people know about this place, which is why it's my favorite spot to hang out," Shekhawat chuckled.

"So, you always come here alone?" Kate asked curiously.

"Of course, yes," Shekhawat replied with a wide smile.

"You're quite the genius loner then. Isn't it boring to sit alone here?" Kate commented.

"Sometimes... it is, but I've learned to live this way," Shekhawat replied in a serious tone.

"How did things go with Meera?" Kate inquired.

"We got to know each other better back in military college," Shekhawat took a sip of his coffee.

"So, you two were seeing each other... like dating?" Kate asked.

"Yeah, sort of dating," Shekhawat confirmed.

"I figured I should give it a shot... Every evening we'd meet at the basketball court, play for an hour, then head to the shopping complex. That routine lasted for months until I was posted to my battalion at Tenga," Shekhawat reminisced.

"Wow, must have been quite a memory," Kate said, holding her coffee mug.

"It was... until I joined my battalion and lost touch with her due to being completely off the grid. The rest, well, you know about me... So, it was like waking up after a week in the military hospital in Tawang after the chinese ambush incident I narrated to you," Shekhawat continued.

"Hi Meera... Yashvardhan here. I love you and I missed you so much," I said to her, overflowing with emotions and at the same time, tears were rolling down my eyes too.

"Hi Yashvardhan... I need to tell you something," Meera said, sounding regretful.

"...Go on," I replied, sensing her seriousness.

"I met someone a few months ago, and we have a connection... we're dating now," Meera confessed.

"And who is this someone?" I asked, my tone devoid of emotion.

"He's a fighter pilot... We've been together for five months now," she replied, as if comparing me to her boyfriend.

"Meera... I thought we were dating... I love you, and hearing this breaks my heart," I admitted.

"Yashvardhan, I understand, but we have to be practical... He's also the son of Dad's friend, and we're planning to get engaged next month. I'm sorry, and my father would never approve of us... You know, family differences," Meera explained.

"Yes, there are... I come from a middle-class family, but I'll work hard for us, for you and me... We can build a simple, happy life together. Trust me, Meera, I've loved you since our school days," I tried to persuade her, but it was futile.

"Yashvardhan, it's not about status... There's nothing in common between our families," Meera concluded.

"Yeah, go ahead... Best of luck for your new life, Meera," I hung up. That day, I swore to focus solely on myself and closed the chapter on Meera forever.

"So, she dumped you?" Kate laughed.

"Why are you laughing? I find it rather rude," Shekhawat replied, uninterested.

"Oh, I'm just glad she did... Otherwise, she'd be here, and I'd never have gotten to know you so well. She probably would have been overprotective... That's how women are," Kate commented.

"Oh, I see..." Shekhawat chuckled. "Yeah, you're right. It's all destiny, Kate. You can't force someone to be with you when destiny has other plans," Shekhawat added.

"Seeing my condition, military doctors declared me unfit for further military duties, and I was discharged," Shekhawat continued.

"Must have been tough... What happened to you, Major?" Kate asked.

"I got severe frostbite from being under snow for too long. The doctors said it would take over a year for me to recover fully, and any extra physical strain could worsen my condition. So, I was sent to the Research and Referral hospital in Delhi, where I stayed for eighteen months until I was finally discharged," Shekhawat explained.

"Eighteen months?" Kate was shocked.

"Yes, and trust me, it wasn't boring. I found a way to contribute," Shekhawat said excitedly.

"How?" Kate asked, curious.

"One morning, while walking in the hospital garden, I helped a blind man find his way back to his ward. I learned he was a war veteran who lost his eyes in the 1999 Kargil conflict. Inside the ward, I saw many others suffering from similar conditions," Shekhawat shared with Kate.

"What did you do then?" Kate asked, intrigued.

"I developed a smart stick for blind people, which detects obstacles and alerts the user with sound signals. I made about two hundred of them and donated them to the hospital," Shekhawat said proudly.

"That's a wonderful humanitarian act, Major. You're a good man," Kate exclaimed.

"It truly was, Kate," Shekhawat replied with a smile.

By this time, a few more couples had arrived at the café.

Kate glanced out of the window and noticed something that caught her attention.

"Aww, look at that cute little puppy," Kate exclaimed.

Shekhawat looked outside as well.

"It seems the little pup is hungry," Kate added.

"Probably," Shekhawat replied.

"Let's rescue the little angel," Kate said as she got up and walked out of the café.

Upon seeing this, Shekhawat followed her to the door of the café. Kate crossed the road, picked up the puppy, cradled it in her arms, and began to pet it. Suddenly, a flash of light caught her attention. The next moment, she lay unconscious, her head resting in a pool of blood. Kate had been struck by a speeding truck—an instant and tragic accident.

Shekhawat froze for a moment upon seeing this, his heart skipping a beat. Gathering himself, he rushed to her side, lifted her gently into his arms, and hurried towards his car.

CHAPTER EIGHT

Accident

"You'll be fine, Kate... Nothing will happen to you," Shekhawat said, holding her hand tightly as tears streamed down his face.

Kate was rushed to the ICU, with doctors and nurses alongside Shekhawat. She lay unconscious on the hospital bed. After a tense moment, she was taken inside the ICU, and Shekhawat stood outside, watching through the glass window, which was soon blocked by curtains.

Shekhawat waited for hours until finally, the doctor emerged from the ICU.

"Doctor, is she alright?" Shekhawat asked anxiously.

"She's breathing and still alive, but her head injuries have left her unconscious. We're hopeful she'll regain consciousness soon, but we can't guarantee it. In cases like this, patients often end up in a coma," the doctor informed him solemnly.

"When she wakes up, you can take her home," the doctor added.

Shekhawat was permitted to enter.

"Sir, she's in critical condition... severe head injuries and a fractured left leg. Once she wakes up, you can take her home," the nurse informed him as she headed towards the ICU exit.

"Ma'am, can you tell me when she might regain consciousness?" Shekhawat asked, stopping the nurse.

The nurse turned to him and replied, "Normally, it takes six to seven hours if everything is normal... But given her condition, we can't be certain," before leaving the ICU.

"Sir, it's been more than six hours now. I'd advise you to go home for tonight. If there's any improvement, we'll inform you immediately," a senior nurse approached Shekhawat, trying to console him as she recommended leaving Kate at the hospital for the night.

Shekhawat waited outside for over six hours, but seeing no change in Kate's condition, he reluctantly left her there for the night.

Driving back to his villa, tears streamed down his face, his heart aching. Suddenly, a thought struck him. He stopped the car, knowing exactly what to do next.

Without wasting a moment, he rushed to his laboratory, spending the entire night in the basement.

The next morning, Shekhawat sought out the same nurse and hurried towards her.

"How is she now?" he asked.

"There's been no change in her condition," the nurse informed him.

"Can I take her home?" Shekhawat pleaded desperately.

"You can take her home at your own risk. There are formalities to complete before she can be discharged," the nurse explained.

"Alright..." Shekhawat headed to the administration block, completing all necessary paperwork. He then took her home, immediately transferring her to his laboratory located in the villa's basement.

Throughout the day, he stood vigil, meticulously attending to a task he had never undertaken before—using

Kate as the first human subject for his experiment. Initially hesitant, he proceeded out of fear that Kate might never wake up.

At midnight, Shekhawat was half-laid over her side, sitting on a stool beside the bed, when he noticed a movement.

"Kate... Kate... Can you hear me?" Shekhawat called out hopefully.

"Mmm..." Kate slowly opened her eyes, gazing at him and then around the room.

"Kate... Do you know who I am?" Shekhawat asked to confirm her neurological state.

"You're a loner, Major," Kate answered with a faint smile.

Shekhawat was overjoyed to see her awake. He hugged her, tears rolling down his cheeks.

"Kate, get some rest... By morning, you'll be completely fine," he said, gently caressing her head and kissing her forehead as he remained seated beside her.

Early the next morning, Shekhawat brought soup for her.

Quietly approaching, he stood beside her. Seeing her deep in sleep, he placed the bowl on the bedside table.

Shekhawat moved closer, looking at her, and took her hand firmly but gently with both of his, kissing it.

"I won't let anything happen to you, and once you're better, I won't let you go, Kate... My story isn't finished yet, and I'm in love with you. I've already imagined our whole life together. You can't leave like this. I wish I could have said this while you were awake," he confessed emotionally.

With that, Shekhawat left the room. An hour later, Ramveer informed him about Kate. Shekhawat rushed back to her immediately.

"Major, give me your hand," Kate gestured towards him.

Shekhawat looked at her strangely, unknowingly placing his hand in hers.

"I love you too... I heard every word you said to me. I was awake," Kate winked.

Shekhawat blushed and became shy.

"Aww, look at you... You're blushing, Major. That was so sweet of you. No one has ever confessed to me like that before," Kate said emotionally, trying to get out of bed.

"I think your leg isn't quite healed," Kate noticed, struggling with her leg.

"The fracture will take time to heal. And now that you're alright but unable to walk, you're not going anywhere, Kate," Shekhawat exclaimed joyfully.

"Fine, I am not going anywhere, Major," Kate smiled.

... the next morning

"Good morning, Saab ji," Ramveer greeted Shekhawat.

"Hey Ramu, morning... Has madam woken up yet?" Shekhawat asked his butler, inquiring about Kate.

"I haven't checked yet, Saab ji. I'm about to take her coffee," Ramveer replied, watering the saplings in the garden when he noticed Shekhawat entering the villa after his morning jog.

"Don't worry, I'll take it to her," Shekhawat said, heading toward the kitchen.

He stood at the partially open door of Kate's room, watching her sleep peacefully. Her hair cascaded over her face, catching the morning light like moonbeams through tree leaves. Shekhawat found himself lost in his thoughts until Kate stirred and noticed him standing there.

"Kate... Are you awake?" Shekhawat asked, holding two coffee mugs.

"Yes... come in, I'm up," Kate replied, propping herself up in bed, a pillow behind her back and another under her fractured leg. She wore a silky cream tank top and black silky shorts.

Shekhawat stepped into the room with a smile. "Good morning, Kate... Here's your coffee." He placed the mugs on the side table and drew back the curtains.

Kate took a mug, smiling. "So you make coffee too?"

"I do, but you should thank Ramveer for this one," Shekhawat winked.

"Are you ready for Christmas Eve?" he asked, excitement in his voice.

"Yay!" Kate exclaimed joyfully.

"Come here, Major... come to me," Kate called him in a sensual tone.

Shekhawat moved closer, sitting beside her, his expression curious. Before he could speak, Kate leaned in and kissed him softly, then more intensely, her hands resting on his shoulders. In the heat of the moment, Shekhawat accidentally pressed his leg against her injured one.

"Ouch... careful!" Kate winced in pain, pulling back, but they both burst into laughter.

"You're a moment-spoiler," Kate teased.

"Sorry..." Shekhawat grinned, moving closer again. Kate playfully resisted before pulling him toward her, locking eyes with him. He kissed her deeply, and the room filled with their shared warmth.

"Saab ji... breakfast is ready," Ramveer called out from outside the closed door.

"... Scoot up," Kate said, trying to gather herself.

"Shush... it's closed, Kate," Shekhawat whispered, teasing her with his tongue on her earlobe.

"You're turning me on, Yash..." Kate murmured seductively.

"Am I?" Shekhawat asked with a laugh, breaking the moment's tension.

He stood up, switched off the room lights, and drew the curtains closed. Back beside her, he reached for the bedside lamp, turning it on. As he gazed at her, desire flickered in his eyes. Slowly, he pulled up her top and slid down her underpants, savoring the sight of her. Kate blushed, her eyes meeting his in a silent exchange.

He turned off the lamp, and the room plunged into darkness. Shekhawat moved closer, his face resting against her bosom, inhaling her scent. His hands traveled down her thighs, lifting her closer to him. Kate wrapped her legs around his waist, surrendering completely. She kissed his shoulders and chest, leaving love bites on his neck. Their passionate encounter lasted for over an hour, leaving them both breathless.

"I'm going to take a shower... See you at breakfast," Shekhawat whispered, kissing her ear before leaving the room.

Kate lay in bed, wrapped in a white sheet, looking like an angel.

"Tell me about your last encounter with Meera," Kate asked as she tore into a French toast with her cutlery.

"Why are you so worried about Meera? You should be more worried about that wheelchair you're in," Shekhawat joked.

"Tell me..." Kate demanded, trying to hit him with her fork.

"Okay, okay," Shekhawat laughed, dodging her playful attack.

CHAPTER NINE

The Shocking Encounter

Yash leaned back in his chair, a faint smile playing on his lips as he began recounting the story to Kate.

"You know, Kate, life has a funny way of bringing things full circle. A few months ago, I found myself back in Bangalore, at the headquarters of an IT company I'd recently acquired. It was a surreal moment for me, stepping into that place, knowing how far I'd come from my days as a struggling soldier trying to find my place in the world.

As I walked through the lobby, taking in the buzz of the place, I spotted someone I hadn't seen in years—Meera. Someone I was once very close to. But during my low phase, when I was just starting my career in the army, she left me. Moved on with someone else, someone she thought was better suited to give her the life she wanted.

She didn't recognize me at first. I guess the years had changed me more than I realized. But when she did, the surprise on her face was almost amusing. She quickly introduced me to one of her male friends, Rohan, this flashy guy who was clearly proud of himself. He shook my hand with a kind of arrogant smile, the kind that says, 'I'm way better than you.'

Rohan asked me what I was doing these days, probably expecting me to say something unimpressive. I kept it vague, telling him I'd been keeping busy. Meera chimed in, asking what brought me to the company. She had no idea that I owned the place now.

Before I could answer, Mr. Kumar, the Managing Director, walked in with a group of executives. When he saw me, he practically beamed and came straight over to greet me.

'Major Yashwardhan Singh Shekhawat! It's an honor to finally meet you in person,' he said, loud enough for half the lobby to hear. Seeing Rohan and Meera standing alongside, he added, "I trust our employees are treating you well."

You should have seen the looks on Meera and Rohan's faces, Kate. They were completely stunned. I could see the wheels turning in their heads, trying to process what was happening. Mr. Kumar went on to introduce me as the new owner of the company, praising my military background and my business acumen. It was clear to Meera that I wasn't just some old classmate anymore.

Meera was at a loss for words. I could see her struggling to find something to say, but I didn't want to make it any harder on her than it already was. So I just smiled and told her it was nice catching up.

As I walked away, leaving them standing there, I couldn't help but feel a sense of closure. Life had taken us down different paths, and I had no bitterness left. If anything, I was grateful for the journey. And in that moment, seeing the shock and, yes, the humiliation on their faces, I realized something important. I had moved on long ago, and the man I had become was more than I ever imagined during those tough times.

It wasn't about showing off or proving a point. It was just... life coming full circle."

Yash finished his story, looking at Kate with a peaceful expression. "And that, Kate, was how I ran into an old chapter of my life, only to realize it had long been closed. I guess that's how it goes sometimes, huh?"

"Wow," Kate exclaimed excitedly.

"That was kind of the last nail in the coffin," she added, laughing.

"So, that's it. Are you satisfied now, or do you want to hear more?" Shekhawat asked, teasingly.

"Satisfied? Yes, for now," Kate chuckled, and they both laughed.Meanwhile both finished their breakfast.

Over the next few days, until Kate finally recovered, they spent every moment together, exploring the unexplored and finding joy in each other's company. Their bond grew stronger with each passing day, and a deep connection formed between them. Every evening, they would visit the same café, savoring coffee together as they shared laughter and stories. Kate's mornings began with Shekhawat brewing coffee for her, his voice filling the room as he narrated more anecdotes and incidents from his life. Each day felt like a new chapter in the story they were writing together.

CHAPTER TEN

The Last Day

The sun was just beginning to dip below the horizon, casting a warm, golden hue over the landscape as Kate stood by the window of her room, gazing out at the serene surroundings that had become so familiar over the past few days. It was her last day at Shekhawat's villa, and a wave of mixed emotions washed over her.

Kate couldn't help but feel a deep sense of gratitude as she thought back to the moments she had shared with Shekhawat. His stories of valor, his journey from a dedicated army officer to a successful entrepreneur, and the unexpected but undeniable bond that had formed between them. It had been an experience she would cherish forever.

As she packed her belongings, she found herself pausing frequently, lost in thought. Each item she placed in her suitcase seemed to carry with it a memory—of laughter, of intense conversations, of quiet moments spent in the company of a man she had come to admire deeply. She knew she would miss the easy camaraderie they had developed, the way they had shared parts of their lives that they hadn't shared with anyone else.

But alongside the sadness of leaving was a sense of fulfillment. Kate had come to India to interview Shekhawat for her book, but she was leaving with so much more than just notes and recordings. She was leaving with a newfound respect for the man behind the stories, and with a piece of her heart firmly rooted in this place.

Shekhawat knocked lightly on her door, interrupting her thoughts. "Are you ready?" he asked, his voice soft but tinged with a hint of sadness.

Kate turned to face him, forcing a smile to mask the emotions swirling inside her. "Almost," she replied, her voice wavering slightly.

He stepped into the room and walked over to her, noticing the open suitcase on the bed. "It's been quite a journey, hasn't it?" he said, his tone reflective.

Kate nodded, unable to find the right words. She reached out and took his hand, giving it a gentle squeeze. "I can't thank you enough for everything, Yash," she said, using his first name in a way that had become more natural over the days. "This has been more than just an interview... it's been a life-changing experience."

Shekhawat smiled, though his eyes revealed the same mix of emotions Kate was feeling. "It was a pleasure having you here, Kate. You've reminded me of things I had almost forgotten and made me see my journey through a different lens."

They stood in silence for a moment, neither wanting to break the spell of their connection. Finally, Kate took a deep breath and released his hand. "I guess it's time," she said, her voice barely above a whisper.

Shekhawat nodded, stepping back to give her space to close her suitcase. "I'll walk you to the helipad," he offered, his tone gentle.

As they walked through the villa one last time, Kate took in every detail, committing it to memory. The house had come to feel like a second home, and leaving it felt like leaving a part of herself behind.

At the entrance, Ramveer was waiting with the car to helipad, his usual cheerful demeanor slightly subdued. "Safe travels, madam," he said with a respectful nod.

"Thank you, Ramveer," Kate replied, her voice warm but tinged with sadness.

The car came to a stop at the helipad, and Shekhawat escorted Kate to the helicopter that would take her to Delhi International Airport for her night flight to California.

Shekhawat opened the chopper's door for her, and as she climbed in, she turned to look at him one last time. "Take care, Yash," she said softly, her eyes glistening with unshed tears.

"You too, Kate," he replied, his voice steady but his expression betraying the emotions he was holding back.

In the soft glow of the setting sun, the helicopter's blades whirred to life, ready to take Kate back to her world. As she stood beside Shekhawat, a bittersweet smile on her lips, she couldn't help but reflect on the past few weeks. What had started as an interview had blossomed into something much deeper—a connection that neither of them had anticipated.

They embraced, a moment of shared understanding passing between them. It was a farewell, but also an acknowledgment of what they had shared—a bond that, though fleeting, had left an indelible mark on both of them.

As Kate boarded the helicopter, she took one last look at Shekhawat, standing tall and resolute. The man she had come to know was far more than just a soldier or a successful entrepreneur. He was a man who had faced the deepest valleys of life and had risen above them, carrying his scars with grace and dignity.

The helicopter lifted off, and as the distance between them grew, Kate felt a pang of longing. But it was tempered by a sense of fulfillment. She had come to write a story, but she was leaving with so much more—a story that had touched her own heart.

Shekhawat watched until the helicopter disappeared into the horizon, a quiet resolve settling over him. Life would go on, as it always did, but the memories of these days would stay with him, tucked away in a corner of his heart.

As the night enveloped him, Shekhawat turned back toward his villa, a small smile playing on his lips. This chapter had ended, but he knew that life, with all its unpredictability, would always have more to offer. And whatever came next, he was ready to face it.

Kate, soaring high above, looked down at the receding landscape, feeling a strange mix of emotions. She was leaving, but a part of her would always remain in that villa, in the stories shared, and in the bond forged with Shekhawat.

And so, their paths diverged, but with a shared understanding that some connections, though brief, are meant to last a lifetime.

Epilogue

Months had passed since Kate's departure, and life had resumed its steady rhythm for Shekhawat. His days were filled with meetings, new business ventures, and occasional reflections on the stories that had shaped his journey. Yet, amidst all the success and the relentless pace of his life, there was one memory that lingered—his time with Kate.

One crisp autumn morning, as Yash was reviewing plans for a new project in his office, his phone buzzed with an international call. He picked it up, expecting a business inquiry, but the voice on the other end caught him off guard.

"Yash, it's Kate."

Her voice, warm and familiar, instantly brought a smile to his face. They had kept in touch, exchanging emails and brief calls, but this one felt different. After a moment of catching up, Kate revealed the reason for her call.

"I'm coming back to India," she said, her tone filled with excitement. "I have a new project, and I was hoping we could meet again."

Yash's heart skipped a beat. The thought of seeing Kate again stirred something deep within him—anticipation, curiosity, and a sense of unfinished business. They had shared so much during her last visit, yet there was still more to explore, more stories to tell.

www.ingramcontent.com/pod-product-compliance
Lightning Source LLC
Chambersburg PA
CBHW022025150726
47990CB00002B/813